BAYLESS

By

Anne Sweazy-Kulju

Bayless

Published in the United States of America
ISBN: 978-0-9995522-8-5

For My Daughter,

My motivation, my reason for everything.

Also by Anne Sweazy-Kulju:

The Thing with Feathers, 2012
BODIE, 2013
Grog Wars, 2015
Grog Wars Dos 2017

ACKNOWLEDGEMENTS

Many thanks to my friend, cheerleader and rainmaker, Bill (Fred) Rotzien. My sincere gratitude goes to Richard Bayless for trusting me with his grandfather's story. My thanks to members of Lincoln City and Bend, Oregon Na-No-Wri-Mo groups (National Novel Writing Month) for their encouraging notes during the 2016 November challenge. It did make the difference.

Chapter 1

Wheaton, Missouri

October 11, 1872

"Can I see 'em?" His broad hand reached for the ribbon, the damned double-knotted ribbon, that sheltered Maggie's breasts.

"No, you may not." She slapped his hand away, giggling. She could barely make out his chiseled silhouette in the darkness of the barn. She tucked her legs under her a bit tighter and shivered. The evenings were starting to get some October chill to the air. Just two weeks earlier, it was still warm enough for late corn and tomatoes. Maggie relished the aroma of the small barn and took in breaths filled with fresh hay, polished leather, and newly oiled machinery.

"You said you'd marry me but you won't let me see them?" He was shaking his head and Maggie could see dark curls bouncing. "Can I touch 'em, then?" He paused his hand in front of her.

She couldn't see Jim's mouth but she could feel him smiling at her. "I am sure you *can*—"

"I can?" He rushed to interrupt her.
"But no, you *may* not." She brushed his hand away.
"Come on, Maggie, just one time—and I won't look, I promise. Give me a swell memory to keep me warm on the trail at night."

Margaret Ellen Morris, daughter of a local Baptist preacher, Daniel Morris, considered that. She did want to gain some assurance that Jim would come back for her. She shivered again, not because of the cold this time, but because she knew her father would marry her to the lone son of Silas Biggs, should Jim choose not to return to her, and Wheaton, Missouri.

James Bayless could just make out Maggie's generous mouth. She was biting a tiny piece of her lower lip. It was a mannerism he loved. It usually meant she was yielding… "How 'bout just one of them? Come on, Maggie."

"Well… Father says he will marry me to the man who can buy me the farm on Shoal Creek for a wedding gift. It's the admiration of the entire county, and father wants it for me."

"You got it. I am going to buy you that farm, Maggie."

"Father says he lost my mother to poverty but he will not lose me. He said you could never support a wife with part time work at the mercantile and delivering the mail. You win foot races at festivals, I know. But they pay winners with ribbons and free pie. You cannot support a family on a couple of racing ribbons and free pie, Jimmy."

"I know—"

"You said you will marry me when you return, but that means you have to come home with gold, and plenty of it."

"I know what I said and I meant it. Now, Maggie, just so I don't go getting myself slapped, do I have permission to reach inside—"

James never finished the thought. The little barn shook as though it would topple right off the foundation. The sound that followed a half-beat later was the most thunderous he had ever heard— and their little corner of the Ozarks hears its share of thunder.

Maggie screamed in surprise. She gathered her sweater over her shoulders and bolted for the barn doors. James slid open the door and they peered out into the twilight of early evening.

"Oh, no. Jim…is Old Boone's cabin on fire?" She placed a hand over her mouth as though silencing herself could somehow make the tragedy untrue.

"I think so, but that was much too big an explosion for a kerosene stove. Boone's cabin is tiny. I cannot figure what could have happened."

Maggie was openly crying now, with tears brimming over pale green eyes, and running right down and between the beautiful breasts Jim had still not seen or held. "Do you think Old Boone was inside?" she cried.

"I don't know, Maggie. Come on." He pulled her by the arm down the hill to the street, and then down toward the main intersection of town, where other townsfolk were already gathering.

The Reverend Richardson of the local Bible Church nodded to Margaret and James. "They are saying Old Boone was inside when the cabin blew. If it's true, I don't suppose there will be any of Boone Davies left to bury, I am a'feared to say." He crossed himself. "One of his clay soldering dams sailed through my church window at the other end of the street."

Jim stared at the Reverend a long moment. "What could have happened? Boone's just a tinker...what in the devil was he melting in those molds of his, besides solder?"

The Reverend shrugged and shook his head sadly. He looked up when Silas Biggs approached. Silas was a big man, over six-feet tall, and handsome as a razorback hog. He was plenty wealthy, but apparently not wealthy enough to suit him. Rumors thronged that Silas had set his sights on acquiring still more neighboring properties—homes belonging to families who had fallen behind in their taxes since the war ended. He was not a man well liked among the denizens of Wheaton, and he could not care less about the matter.

"Guess we know who the firewood thief was." He growled as he lit the end of a cheroot and inhaled the sickly sweet smoke.

Murmurs ceased and all eyes turned toward Biggs. "What do you mean by that, Silas? What have you done?" The Reverend asked.

"I'll tell you what. I had me a firewood varmint. Someone was stealing firewood from my woodpile every night, of late. I know that varmints don't care much for the scent of powder, so I bore a few holes in a few of them logs and filled 'em up with black powder. Then I covered the holes with tree sap and set 'em on the pile, no one the wiser." He took another smoke, caring little about the fact folks were staring at him. He nodded toward the still burning remains of Boone Davies' sad, unpainted shack. "Like I said before, guess we know who the firewood varmint was."

"Good Heavens, Silas. Old Boone was just a poor tinker who didn't have much or need much. He's been tinkering tin pots and kettles around these parts for years. The poor man had no wealth to his name, save the smile he always wore, some solder and the clay for his dams. You, on the other hand, are the richest man in town and maybe the whole county. You couldn't find generosity enough in your heart, Silas, to give a nice old man a warm fire for his modest cabin?" Reverend Richardson asked.

"What are you talking about?" He waved his hand toward the burning shack. "I gave him a fire for his cabin, all right." Biggs tossed the remnant of his cheroot to the ground and stomped on it. He turned and walked away.

The Reverend shouted after him. "There was a man in that cabin you destroyed with your booby-trap, Silas Biggs. You killed a man, not a varmint. You will be judged."

"I didn't kill anybody, Reverend Richardson. Old Boone blew his own self up. And I couldn't give a Tinker's dam," Biggs tossed over his shoulder, laughing hearty at his own joke.

James looked at Maggie. He reached and swiped moisture from her cheek. "Your father, he wouldn't really marry you into that family, would he?"

She sniffed and dabbed at her eyes, then turned to her sweetheart. "Come back for me, Jimmy. Don't dare think to abandon me." She buried her head in his chest and sobbed.

Lem was about to destroy the small House of God, and perhaps his family jewels in the process, just for fun. "Watch this!" He hollered at Jim when he saw his friend walk through the open door.

Lem was paid a dollar to collect and stack all of the chairs and sweep the floor after services each week for Reverend Richardson, but he had left a single row of the whitewashed chairs stretching wall-to-wall in the modest church. Jim surveyed the scene and knew exactly what his friend was planning to do.

"Don't do it, Lem. You're going to maim yourself and maybe die, and I cannot spare you at this time, partner. We need to go to Colorado and dig for gold."

Lem laughed aloud and pushed an unruly wave of ginger hair back from his freckled forehead. His thick mop needed clipping, but Lem liked wearing it long almost as much as he liked saving money on haircuts. "You're a feeble-minded cracker, my long, tall friend. The calendar only just flipped to October. Nobody sets out for the Rockies in late fall. You must have caught gold fever."

Lem turned and focused on the row of chairs, revved up his nerves and momentum, and then ran and jumped atop the first chair in the row. He proceeded to jump from one chair to the next, one foot quickly pushing off a chair, while the other foot reached for the next in the row. To Jim, Lem looked like one of those lumberjacks running across a flotilla of logs, but not as smoothly.

Lem yelled at his friend, "Are you watching me ride this chair gauntlet? Are you watching this?" until he reached the middle of the row. There, Lem's foot pushed off from one of the chairs a bit too hard and the chair toppled. Lem toppled with it; a few of the wooden folding chairs breaking his fall.

"And you just had the gumption to call me a feeble-minded cracker, you crazy fool? Did you bust anything?" Jim asked.

"My ass. I think I busted my ass, Jim." He got up rubbing his bum and chuckling.

"I mean did you break any of the church's property? I don't want to have to fix a bunch of chairs before we can leave for Colorado."

Lem dragged fingers through unruly strawberry hair and adjusted his waist overalls. He started picking up chairs and checking them for damages. Every once in a while he would rub the left side of his fanny and moan. Jim stepped over to help him.

"Are you being serious about leaving right away?" Lem handed a chair to Jim to stack. "I mean I know I've been bugging you to go, but I figured we would go in the spring, like normal prospectors."

"Maggie's father turned me down, Lem. I cannot fault him, I have no property, no wealth—"

"No job," his friend interjected.

"I have a job."

"Yeah, but, working for your brother, and only a couple of days each week. That ain't really a steady job—or at least not enough of one. And your horse does most of the work for you, for crying out loud. You tell Indy to go and get the mail, and she takes herself to the mercantile for you."

"I am aware. I trained her. In any case, thusly the journey to Colorado to find gold, fool. Did you hit your head when you took your spill?" Jim complained.

Lem laughed. He handed over the last chair; happily not a one of them had broken under his weight. "I did hit my head, as a matter of fact. But see?" He knocked on his noggin. "I got a hard shell. No bumps. Nothing there, at all." He grabbed a wide floor mop and began pushing it back and forth across the empty floor. "Jimmy, if you're serious, you know I'll be the bacon to your grits. Let's grab up some pans and picks at the mercantile and hit the trail, already. Won't do us any good to wait."

James Bayless gave his best friend in the world a smile, wide as a country mile. "You know me. I have already assembled almost everything we'll need, Lemmy. We can bug out by Sunday, after church, if you're certain you have a mind to do it."

"Well then, here we go, I suppose." Lem propped the big mop in the corner and followed his friend out the doors. He reached the bottom step, sucker-punched Bayless in the ribs and yapped, "race you to the end?" The two young men removed their shoes and socks and lined up side-by-side. Lem, who measured five-feet and eleven inches in height, was a full five inches shorter than the long-legged friend beside him.

"Go!" Lem yelled. They took off like cats with tails on fire, sprinting toward the main street intersection that was a couple hundred or so yards to their east. It was an easy win for James.

"You're getting faster, Lem." Jim told him.

"I thought so, too. But so are you. Dang, Jimmy, it's too bad you can't make any kind of a living just being a fast man."

James Bayless was not just a fast man. He was also a world-class ultra runner. But, while there was much respect and prestige for such athletes, there was no money to be made there, either.

The sport was introduced to Midwest Native Americans, in particular the Osage Nation and the Hopi Indians, by Scottish immigrants hundreds of years earlier. James ran because he liked it. Running kept him fit and it took him places; following trails, pushing across rivers and over mountains, and ultimately realizing destinations and panoramas seldom revealed to the ordinary man. Jim's was a prowess and legacy that belonged to the tribal running messengers of hundreds—perhaps even thousands of years before him. In fact, the junction of the North Missouri Railroad at Macon and the Kansas state line was finished the previous year. James, wearing reinforced moccasins and carrying nothing save some water and a few cans of gruel made from parched corn he sweetened with sugar, ran almost two hundred miles over three days just to witness the train's maiden journey.

Chapter 2

"What are you doing, sitting there drinking coffee?" Lem Hassen yelled through the open door at his partner. He flailed his arms like a crazy man in mass confusion. Lem was one of those larger-than-life men who amplified everything he said with grand motions and exaggerated facial expressions.

"Uh, it is my day off at the mercantile, I sent Indy for the mail, and I thought I would enjoy a good cup of Jo. I have packed some coffee for our journey but trust me, it ain't gonna taste as good as this."

"Tell me you're funnin'. You are, aren't you? We're up in about 15 minutes, Fly. Tex and Ark nearly skunked Uncle Bean and Lawman, and they did it in less than forty-five minutes. You plus me, we are now in the finals. Grab your mallet and let's go."

James bottomed-up his mug and walked it over to the wooden sink, pumped some water through it and hung it on a hook to dry. He wiped his hands on a plain white dishcloth. He turned to Lem. "We leave in two days. You really want to spend one of them playing croquet with a bunch of old men in town?"

"What?" cried a dramatic Lem, his arms and fingers sprawling. "Hell yes, I do. I want that trophy before I leave this life." He brusquely passed by his friend, stomped through the living area to a small bedroom off a short hall, and began rummaging though athletic gear hung up and resting in one corner. He picked up one of the customized short-handled mallets the two friends had made together and carried it out to the small kitchen. Every man made his own croquet mallet; it was a tedious process to get it just right, and whoa to anyone who messed with another player's mallet.

It started with a rolling pin. They sawed off the ends with great care to cut them true, without any slant. They bored a deep hole at the center of the roller and glued a mop handle into the hole. Most folks cut the handle down to about two feet, but Jim stood six feet and three inches tall; they cut his handle down to two and a half feet in length. The shortened handles resulted in bending players down close to the ball in order to strike it. Lem and Jim finished their customized mallets by stretching thin pieces of leather over both ends of the perpendicular rolling pins, which provided smooth, flat surfaces for striking the hard rubber croquet ball.

"I didn't know it meant so much to you, Lem. All right, I'll go. But we're probably walking the half-mile to town. I already sent Indy to fetch the mail for me."

"When did you ever walk anywhere?" Lem laughed and began removing his shoes and socks.

The croquet court, a large rectangle of packed sand, stood at the west end of Wheaton's Main Street. Strong metal wickets, six and one-half inches wide, had been set in concrete so they couldn't be moved by one of the hard-hit black rubber balls. Rocky Comfort had a similar court, and Cassville had a court, too, albeit a bit smaller and without concrete stabilization.

Lem Hassen, nicknamed, "Ginger", and James Bayless, nicknamed, "Fly", would be "rifling the skunk's nest against Bird and Archer in a match for the Barry County Croquet Championship." Barney Fagan wrote in his report, *Echoes From the Court*, for the Wheaton Journal. Fagan allowed his young son to sit on the bench with him and watch the all-important match. It was a rare occasion, as the games were supposed to be off limits to women and children.

"Sit still, don't talk, don't whittle, don't cough, and don't fart." Fagan reminded the boy.

"And make myself invis-wable," the youngster piped in.

"Invisible, yes." Fagan put a finger to his lips, and that was the last the men heard or took notice of the boy.

A spectator, one of the folks who lived on the outskirts of town who Bayless delivered mail to, clapped Jim on the back and told him, "I can't barely wait for the Harvest Festival, Jimmy. I got ya this year. Yessir, I got me a fast horse and he's goin' to win me my money back. Yee-hee." He yelled in Jim's ear.

Jim shook his neighbor's hand. "Good to see you, Hock. I have to deliver some bad news to you, though. I ain't gonna be here for the festival this year. I am heading for Colorado gold, my friend. I'm leaving day after tomorrow. Lem's coming with me." He added.

"Dang, Jimmy, in October? And don't tell me you're aiming to run the distance. It's madness, son, and maybe suicide."

"Good golly, no. We're neither mad nor suicidal, Hock. We'll be taking our mounts to the train at Macon, and riding the rails through Kansas, all the way to the Colorado border. Tracks aren't there beyond the border yet, so we'll ride Indy and Riff to the gold fields near Pueblo, I suppose. Folks say they're just picking nuggets off the ground in some places; a man doesn't even need a pick. Don't worry for us. I figure we'll be back 'fore Christmas."

Hock Benson frowned at the two young men. His eyes held a strange mix of excitement and concern. "I hope your strike is rich, boys. Lord knows if anyone could do it, I believe Jim Bayless could…and you, Lem, of course. Just make certain you have money for a safe train ride home, boys. You don't want to be riding your horses unescorted across Indian country. They ain't all tamed."

The attendance of Fagan's son ensured this particular match would be unique, but Bayless made it rare for one more reason. If you were "skunked" in a croquet match, your opponent made it all the way through the course of wickets before you ever cleared a single wicket with your ball. On that Friday afternoon in October, Arlie Noman, aka Bird, and his son, Archer, were doubly glad that Mr. Fagan always used players' nicknames when he wrote for the Journal. His account of this particular weekend's event would report how Ginger and Fly applied the skunk oil liberally to the Bird/Archer team, and in less than thirty minutes. That caused "Lawman" to begin telling Wheaton fans that the Championship may not have been won legally, which caused Fagan and his newspaper some grief. The long-established rule for the croquet courts of Barry County was that a legal game lasted 45 minutes. Bird and Archer were mopped up in about twenty-five minutes and so the match was illegal, Bird contested.

Fans argued that since Bird never even hit the ball, and his son only hit a ball one time, just how were their opponents expected to draw out the play? By walking backwards or playing with hands tied, they asked? In the end, the folks of Wheaton had to draw their own conclusions about the match, but the trophy went home with Lem Hassen, just the same.

Every girl dreams of being sneaked up on from behind by a boy she knows from school, especially with her hair tied up in a scarf, and while brushing excrement from the floors of rabbit cages. At least that must have been what Maggie Morris' father had been thinking when he sent Silas Biggs' son down to the rabbit barn to find her.

She was being careful not to let her hand get too close to the mama rabbit or her babies while she cleaned out the cage. If her hand passed by too close, the mama rabbit would try to pounce on her and scratch her up. "Ow!" she exclaimed, withdrawing her hand from the cage.

"Looks like she got you good. Nasty things. I'll take her out and break her neck for ya." Buddy Biggs offered, startling Maggie.

"Oh, Buddy. I didn't know anyone else was around." She blotted away a thin bloody scratch. "No, she is just protecting her young. I won't punish her for being a good mama."

"Oh." Buddy looked about the small barn without interest. He shuffled his feet but made no other attempt at conversation.

The silence grew uncomfortable. Finally, Maggie tried to fill the void. "Did you need a meat rabbit, Buddy? I can deliver one to the butcher for you to pick up later, or you can take a live one and... I apologize but I cannot bring myself to..."

"Oh. Okay." Buddy answered her, staring at his shoes.

"You know, Buddy, once you have purchased one of my rabbits, it means you find me charming and funny, and a friend forever." She smiled pretty at Buddy and wondered about what his life must be like, alone in that austere cabin with a cruel and withholding father. It was probably fairly pitiful, she imagined.

After more silence, Maggie asked her visitor outright if there was something else he needed. This sent Buddy shuffling from one foot to the other, hemming and hawing, until finally blurting out, "I'm supposed to ask, will you come to the house for eats with me an' my pa on Sunday?"

Maggie was flummoxed by his offer after she had just branded him a *friend*, but she knew Buddy Biggs could not be expected to comprehend social finesses and nuances. Maggie's father, a preacher by profession and farmer by necessity, once joked that Buddy was told by the angels to get into the line for brains, but poor Buddy thought he heard 'trains' and ran away shouting he wouldn't like the ride.

"Gee, Buddy, that is a very nice offer, but I am no longer free for visits from other men. I am engaged and will soon be married." She answered.

"To Bayless?" He asked.

"Yes, to James Bayless." She watched Buddy Biggs digest the information. He seemed neither surprised nor dismayed by what she had said.

"Oh." Buddy stared vacantly at the rabbits, neatly stacked in their fastidiously clean cages. The bunnies stared back, while they chewed on clumps of fresh hay or alfalfa that Margaret had stuffed inside wire holders hanging inside each pen.

After another awkward silence, Maggie sighed a bit theatrically and wiped her brow. "Boy, I don't know how I will get all of these cages cleaned today. I seem to be running out of daylight." She told him.

Buddy finally seemed to get the idea that Maggie was too busy to chat. "I guess I will go then. I will let pa know he can have a rabbit for his Sunday dinner, if he wants one." Buddy Biggs turned around and shuffled out the barn doors.

Maggie looked up at the house and could see her father sitting on the front porch trying to appear as though he were not watching the meeting between Buddy and her. "Oh, Father." She shook her head and went back to cleaning cages.

John Bayless threw his Stetson to the ground and swore. "This is a fool thing to do, and you must know it, Jim. What the heck is wrong with you that everything has to be so dag-nab right-now? You have to run everywhere, fast. You have to marry a girl, fast. You have to make a fortune, fast. Jimmy, life is supposed to be paced, measured. It isn't meant to go fast."

"For some it's fleeting. Look what happened to Old Boone." James argued with his older brother.

"You need to slow down. Come to college with me, if you really want to earn a fortune. It will sure take some time and hard work for us, but we will return to Wheaton set for life as men of commerce. Then you marry your girl and start a family."

"Sounds nice, John."

"I was hoping you would agree. Now, come on Jimmy, let's quit this Colorado gold balderdash, and we'll discuss college and your future over Sunday dinner."

"I mean it sounds nice for you, John. It sounds perfect. But you have always had everything worked out for yourself. Good golly, you have wanted to be a banker since you were knee-high to a fly. The Barry County Bank in Cassville never squeezed its lending money so tight as you. You charged *me* interest if I borrowed part of your allowance. You weren't even ten years old."

"So, what do you want, then, Jim?"

Jim tied off the last pack hanging on Indy's haunches and turned to face his brother. "Maggie. I want Maggie, John. But her pa is set on marrying her off to someone with substantial wealth, and Silas Biggs has come calling on her—maybe for his son, maybe for himself; to be honest, I try not to think on that too much. You're a gentleman, John. Tell me, could you honestly see Maggie playing wife to Silas and his slow-witted heir in that dark fortress he calls a cabin? This here," he waved his hand over the bundled mare, "is how I get to keep Maggie. Besides brother, I am not college material."

John Bayless digested his brother's reasoning. He had to look up at his little brother to give him a scowl before stooping to snatch his Stetson wide-brimmed hat out of the dirt. He banged the dust out of it against his thigh until the hat was black again. "I don't think Preacher Morris would do it to his daughter, but I understand your reasoning. I just...it's dangerous and rash, Jim, this thing you want to do--and with Lem Hassen to watch your back? That's just asking for something to go wrong. I sure wish you could think as fast as you can run, Jim. I sincerely don't want you to go."

James Bayless threw his arms around his big brother and bear-hugged him off the ground. He shook him a few times for good measure and told him, "I love you, too, brother," before releasing him.

She lay in her bed, listening to house sounds. She was alone. Their little cabin was cool; the night's fire reduced to embers. But her bed was warm and snuggly and Maggie wriggled with delight. She recalled her dream, a madly *pleasurable* dream. In it, she had envisioned a continuation of Jim's and her meeting of many nights earlier in the big barn. Her dusky Midwest Native American cheeks actually blushed while she recalled her dream, and an evening redone by her imagination. In Maggie's dream, Old Boone had been alive and well, so no tragedy interrupted them.

She was again thinking of Jim when silently, smoothly, her hand slipped beneath her camisole and began lightly playing with her breasts and stiffening nipples; in no time, they darkened with an eager blood supply. Her free hand slipped beneath her bloomers and Maggie moaned with delight. She whispered Jim's name to the heavens and shuddered over and over again.

Maggie tucked a sweaty lock behind her ear. She stared at the ceiling and listened to her heartbeat. The Sunday morning had a reverent hush about it. The only sound was a ticking that radiated from an iron woodstove winding down. Maggie began to pray. *Dear God, I do not know what to do. I want to share such intimacy and delight with Jim, the man I love more than my own life. He's*

Riff and Indy had been with the farrier most of the morning. Both horses needed new shoes for the journey. Lem was finishing packing the remainder of his gear for the trip and would meet Jim at the mercantile at around 2 p.m. Jim had been packed and ready to go since Friday night before, so he could spend every single moment with Maggie on that Sunday.

He had been invited to brunch with both Maggie and her father, Pastor Morris. The Pastor had pitched in and helped Maggie with some of the tasty late-breakfast preparations. He was a charming host to Jim, start-to-finish—he even wished Jim luck. James Bayless, who could certainly spot a bull-shitter, believed the pastor meant it. They shook hands, clapped shoulders, and then the pastor announced that for the remainder of his day, he would be working on a new sermon, down at the little Baptist church. The two lovebirds waved to him out-of-sight. Maggie turned to James with her green eyes dancing. "Come on," she pulled him by the arm toward the horse barn.

Chapter 3

The two friends rode their mounts hard for an hour and then dismounted and walked beside them at a comfortable pace. In this way, they made it to Macon, Missouri in great time. Jim was quiet, pensive. Lem, however, was embarking on the trip of his life. He was a man on a spiritual high and did plenty of talking for both of them, his hands remonstrating wildly, right along.

The two friends camped that night outside of Nevada, Missouri. Lem built a campfire while Jim dug through his pack and located a bundle wrapped in a large white cloth. He unwrapped the towel to reveal a freshly baked loaf of bread, courtesy of Maggie and Pastor Morris. There was cheese to go with it and coffee, too.

"Holy cow, Jimmy. Your girl can look like that *and* bake bread like this? You are one lucky man." Lem took another big bite and groaned with delight.

"You have no idea." Jim answered, staring at the stars above him.

Lem flashed white teeth. "Really? You and Maggie, uh...?"

"Uh, I wouldn't tell you if we had, but no, Lem. I didn't want to." Lem cackled at that, and slapped his knee repeatedly. Jim sighed with exasperation. "I love Maggie—"

"All the more reason..." Lem interrupted him.

"Is that right, Lem? What if I was to get Maggie pregnant and then, for whatever reason, I couldn't make it back to her. What then?"

"Why couldn't you make it back?" Lem asked, dumbfounded.

Jim stared at his best friend. "Lem, you are three years my senior, so I expect you've given this trip considerable, mature deliberation, am I right?"

"Sure, of course. What are you talking about?"

"Lemmy, Come on. We're journeying across the plains. You must know shit could happen to us. There's a chance we might not make it back."

"Again, what are you talking about?" Lem asked.

"We could be attacked by animals, get run down by wild buffalo, or scalped by Indians. Or we might catch winter fever, just to name a few what-could-be's. My brother, John, said the Indians in the area are neither vanquished, nor tamed."

Lem was quiet for a spell. Bayless turned on an elbow to face his friend and tore off another piece of bread. "You know who else is enjoying this bread...at least I hope he is?"

"Who?" Lem answered, mouth full.

"Old Boone." Bayless told him.

"How's that?" Lem was fairly curious about how a dead man might enjoy freshly baked bread. But thinking on it, he decided Maggie's loaf might smell good all the way to heaven.

"Maggie made two loaves. One was for us and one was for Old Boone. She said she learned through her father that, for a time now, Boone had only been able to afford sawdust bread. Maggie felt so horrible about not knowing—that good-hearted woman of mine would have taken him bread every week, if she had known—that she wanted to take a loaf over to the memorial that some folks created for Boone out of his cabin's rubble."

Lem stared at the hunk of bread he held in one hand. "I didn't know that about Boone. Did you?"

"Good golly, no. The man always wore a glad smile and kept another in his grip. I never guessed he lived in such a state. I knew Tinkers didn't garner much in wages, but everyone always fed Boone after he fixed their wares and before turning him loose. Folks knew to do that. Wheaton folks are generous that way. I thought he was okay…actually, I am sorry to admit, I never really thought about Boone at all."

"Yeah, me neither. I don't think it makes us bad people, though, Jim. We didn't know any better about Old Boone."

"I know. I think I could be a better man, though, and I'm going to try, for Maggie. I'll tell you straight, Lem. I am going to be the best man I can possibly be, or I'll die trying."

Lem thought about that a moment. "My ma fixed me the finest Sunday dinner today. Then just before dessert, she starts bawling about never being prouder of me for aiming to make my way in the world—almost set me off my apple dumplings. I swear, Jimmy, I never want to disappoint my ma. I…I want to be a good man, too. I know I got some growin' to do, but I'm willing. I could probably use your help."

"Sure, Lem. I will never quit you, brother." Bayless reached for the coffee pot and refilled both of their tin cups.

Lem nodded at is friend. "Maggie sure is a sweetheart. I hope I find someone like her. Someday, when I have money, maybe I will."

"There's no one else like Maggie." Bayless said.

Lem took a swig of coffee and looked thoughtful. "I always thought the Sawdust Bread folks jawed about during the war was a myth. You know what I'm thinking now?" Without waiting for a reply, Lem continued, "I'm thinking folks still aren't doing too good since the war."

"I think you're right. Nonetheless, nearly the whole town of Wheaton, at one point or another, came out to Boone's cabin and paid respects with flowers and such to a smoking pile of rubble. That kind of bothered me, so I carved Old Boone a proper marker. I finished it with a quote from the British poet, Thomas Hood. Maggie loves him."

"What was the quote?" Lem wanted to know.

James Bayless closed his eyes and pictured the wooden slab in his mind. "It read, 'O God! That bread should be so dear, and flesh and blood so cheap!' Then, of course, Maggie left the loaf at the base of it."

"That was real good of you, Jimmy." Lem paused, then sighed loudly. "I bet someone came and took that loaf of bread off Boone, straightaway."

Kansas City, Missouri

October 18, 1872

Riff didn't much care for the train and Lem didn't feel good about leaving him in the livestock car. Fortunately, the railroad hired ex-cavalry to maintain the mounts and chattel of passengers. A little gratuity would get your horse brushed down for you, and might even net your four-legged friend a sugar cube or some fresh hay. Both men tipped the groom handsomely. They stayed until the last possible moment, but the time had come to nuzzle their horses' faces one last time, and run for the red-painted passenger cars up ahead, before the iron locomotive got to huffing and puffing its black smoke down the tracks.

Millions of flat, parched acres with names like Perryville, Topeka, Silver Lakes and Cross Creek, clacked passed the car window as the train rocked the men silent. After the first day-and-night of travel, Bayless commented to his companion, "they say Buffalo Bill himself was hired last year by the Kansas Pacific Railroad."

"For what purpose?" Lem asked, only half awake. He stretched out a big yawn.

"To feed the railroad builders, and the town of support services that traveled behind them—a town on wheels, they call it."

Lem lifted the brim of his hat and eyed his friend, unsure if he was being hog-wallowed.

Bayless looked him in the eyes, sideways, and nodded. "I'm telling you true. I heard Bill would plug a train car like this one full with shootists, and perch still more men on the roof of the car. When they passed by a herd of buffalo, they were all guns a' blazing. They killed hundreds of buffalo in that way, maybe even thousands."

"Seems unsportsmanlike." Lem grunted. "But I guess there's a lot of responsibility on a hunter who is tasked with feeding an entire town."

"True. But you know what else is true? I haven't seen a single buffalo yet, and we've gone most the way across the state of Kansas."

Lem's mouth fell open and the toothpick he'd been working dropped out. "Not a single one across the whole danged state? What are the natives supposed to eat all winter long? Entire villages will starve."

Bayless shook his head, pondering. "I think the miners and the settlers won't be happy until they have wiped the Red Man out."

Almost to Cheyenne Wells, just inside the Colorado border, the tracks dipped southwest toward Pueblo and stopped. It was the end of the line for the Kansas Pacific Railroad—at least for the time being. Having failed to garner government funds that would carry the tracks further west they simply, and quite abruptly, ended.

Besides a telegraph office, which truth-be-told was not much more than a shack, the town was abandoned. There was a small depot with benches, a saloon, and a blacksmith. The saloon was closed and had been since the keeper, a man named Nielson, was hung for murdering the town's founder and benefactor, Thom Whipple-Hayes.

The man at the small station's ticket window was too happy to tell them the story of Tarn City. Whipple-Hayes, with help from his brother and a few others, incorporated the small town of Tarn, and implemented a ban on the consumption or sale of liquor inside the town limits. After a few years passed, a saloonkeeper named Hoyt Nielson moved to town and set up shop one block northeast of the railroad depot, mere feet outside of the actual township. Soon alcoholism was stealing men Whipple-Hayes had hired to work for him. This, in addition to Whipple-Hayes' personal feelings against liquor, had him railing against the saloon. He called it a bawdy, especially violent, low-down doggery. Nielson took obvious offense and started arguing with Whipple-Hayes. The two men took to shouting insults at each other, when Nielson suddenly brandished a knife and stabbed Whipple-Hayes three times in the chest and stomach. A friend of Nielson's offered him a "get-away horse" immediately after the stabbing, but the horse had more sense than his owner and objected to having a murderer on his back. He bucked the killer off.

Nielson later said his "personal honor code" required a swift and homicidal reply to Whipple-Hayes' ruinous insults. He claimed self-defense. The ticket clerk told Lem and Jim that it only took Judge Reuben Boise a day to try the case, and a jury one hour to return a guilty verdict.

"It was kind of a sad and funny thing to witness. Nielson was drunk as a skunk. He couldn't even walk to the gallows without help. When asked for last words, he could only mumble unintelligible sounds. Men stood him on that trap door, affixed a black cap, dropped a rope over his head, and sprung the door. Nielson fell through it, but he hit the ground with his feet. I guess no one had measured the distance and they cut the rope too long. The Tarn City sheriff and a deputy had to carry Nielson back up the steps, prop him on the door, and put a few twisty knots in the rope to shorten it. All a sudden Nielson piped up with, "So my hell is to suffer my hanging again and again? Didn't even feel it. This hell ain't so bad." He was laughing when they dropped him through again. They got him dead to rights, that time." the ticket man crowed.

"We made it, Jim. We're in Colorado." Lem shouted happily. They were getting ready to ride. It was early morning and cloudy, but the temperatures were already reaching into the upper-seventies. It would make for a muggy trip.

Little flying no-seeums were being a nuisance, but otherwise Colorado looked entirely welcoming. Looking about, however, Jim wasn't seeing any nuggets of gold sitting on the ground waiting for him to pluck them away. He had thought that story too good to be true. But, it didn't matter. James Bayless might be a tad impatient about things, but he was not afraid of a little hard work.

"Say, friends, you look like capable sorts. Perhaps you can help me." The short man who approached extended a hand and Jim shook it. He then pointed to a sad looking mule tied up to a hitching post near the tracks. "I have a mule what fell victim to the loose-mules-and-oxen car. Somehow he succeeded in damaging himself during the ride; he's a jumper. Anyhow, he's got himself a fractured foreleg. He's useless to make the trip with me, I'm afraid."

"I'm not sure how's we can be of help, but we can try." Jim offered. Lem nodded.

"Well, I don't want the greys and coyotes to get him."

"Greys?" Lem repeated.

"Grey wolves; big ones. A few Grizzlies and Black Bear in this area, too, but the latter won't eat him and will try to steer clear of people, mostly. I hear'd there are some small bands of struggling Ute in the area —them's the nice Apache. If someone was of courage and a mind to help them poor Indians with their starvation plight, I would hand over this unfortunate mule— maybe trade it for some pretty beads or something, to make them natives feel alright about it." He looked from Bayless to his friend. "The Conductor tol' me there's a Ute village up the holler two miles, 'fore you get to Boggsville," he pointed toward foothills southwest of their position. "There's a few more villages northwest of here, but they're further up some foothills that are mostly ridge-and-saddle sorts. I don't think Rocky can make 'em before nightfall." Jim could see there were tears in the man's eyes and he immediately felt sad for his fellow traveler; the man had feelings for his mount, "Rocky".

"We're heading that way, mister". Jim pointed southwest. "Ease your mind, we'll take Rocky up the holler for you."

Soon, reigns in hand, Jim paced his gait beside the lame animal. Indy was hitched to Riff, ridden by Lem. It took them less than one hour to arrive at the tiny, impoverished village, but they'd managed to time their visit in the middle of an altercation between the natives and some miners in the area. It looked like the two groups were going to mix it up.

"This ain't any good. Heck, they might just kill each other." Jim said. He strode over and put himself between the main Indian and the main White Man. "We wouldn't want to have any trouble here, men. What's this matter about?"

The miner said he and the native were out hunting in the same place and one shot a vulture and the other shot a turkey. Then he said, "I told the Injun I could take the turkey and he could take the vulture, or he could take the vulture and I would take the turkey."

Bayless squinted at the miner. "I don't think so, friend." He turned to the Indian and asked, "Which one of you shot the turkey".

"My arrow shot the turkey. A rifle shot the vulture." The Indian nodded toward the dead birds on the ground next to the miner.

"We'll flip a coin for the outcome. Heads I win, tails he loses," the miner said.

Bayless had to put a hand on the Indian fella's chest and hold him back. "Hold on, I am going to fix the matter." To the white man, Jim said, "I don't believe he is much interested in your funny coin or test of fools, mister. If you want to steer clear of trouble, you better start talking turkey with him."

The Indian piped up, "Yes, we will talk turkey, now." His friends started chanting, "talk-turkey, talk-turkey, talk-turkey!"

The miner's friends urged him to give up the bird before there was a misfortune of the scalping sort, and he did. The small band of Ute was grateful to Jim and Lem for working the fowl matter out for them, and also for the mule. They gave Jim a red silk scarf in trade. Clearly it was an artifact the impoverished Indians prized. Jim said his girl would fancy it, and tied it to his saddle horn. That seemed to please the Native Americans pretty much. In fact, the Chief told his braves to keep an eye out for the White Man with the red silk, and let other Apache know they are protected friends.

Chapter 4

Foothills East, Near Aria, Colorado

October 23, 1872

"You expect me to believe a woman is running for President of the United States, against General Grant and Horace Greeley?" Lem waved away the idea.

"It's true. Her name is Victoria Woodhull and she wrote a letter to the New York newspapers a year ago announcing it. Then last week, she registered her candidacy." Jim insisted. He turned his face to the mild sun and relished another balmy October day. Winter was coming. But today, it remained an unimaginable abstract for a future time.

"Get out of Dodge! A woman cannot run for President—it's dumb. A woman cannot even vote for herself. Can she?" Lem couldn't tell if Bayless was telling the truth or just having fun with him.

"Women cannot vote, so no, she could not vote for herself. But she is also too young to be President. She is only 34 years old. And, if that's not enough to make you look out for flying pigs, her named running mate doesn't know her and says he has never spoken to her in person or in writing. She never invited him to run on her ticket."

"Who?"

"Her running mate, Frederick Douglass." Jim laughed.

"The former slave turned writer and orator?"

"That's the very one. And here's the funniest slice: Just last week, Frederick Douglass endorsed General Grant for President. Cross my heart and hope to die, Douglass is right now traveling around campaigning for him."

There was only so much Lem Hassen could swallow. "Pull the other leg, Jimmy. It's got bells on." Lem shook his foot out of the stirrup at his friend to emphasize his disbelief. His timing could not have been worse.

⚜ ⚜

The back of his hand came out of nowhere and caught Buddy squarely across the right side of his face. It would most certainly leave a mark. Silas Biggs' son had grown accustomed to his father's demonstrations of displeasure. He kept vowing to one day run away, but run where, and with what?

"How did you invite her to dinner? Were you polite? Did you look at her or at your feet, you dimwit?" Silas charged.

"I dunno." Buddy squeaked.

"You don't know? You don't *know?*" Silas thundered. Even Buddy's poor reflexes told him to duck, but no blow landed that time. "I thought I made it clear to you how important this is to me. All you have to do is court a pretty girl. How hard can that be with her boyfriend three states west?"

"She said she is engaged and she don't want to court no one else. She was real nice. She wanted to give me a fat rabbit for dinner." Buddy sought to soften his father's disappointment.

"She said she was engaged?" Silas sought to control the anger in his voice.

"To Jimmy Bayless." Buddy confirmed.

"Her pa says different. So, I guess we'll just see about it." Silas' eyes held to mean slits. "I want that land, son, and I don't much care what I have to do—or who I have to marry you to, to get it. Are you going to help me, or are you going to act like a circus geek?"

The Prairie Rattlesnake is common to Colorado's foothills year-round, but even more so twice each year—during it's mating season in the spring, and Dove Season in the fall. Surprisingly, these reptiles are on the shy side and try to hide on ledges and under rocks and such, away from man and his ilk. But poor Riff was just as startled as the snake, when his foreleg came down on the far side of a fallen tree snag and woke one of them. That viper leapt several feet into the air at Riff, who responded by rearing up to avoid the strike, perhaps hoping to stomp the snake on the downside. But the act, instead, threw his rider to the ground without ceremony—right next to the very pissed off rattler.

Bayless was quick to react. He jumped from his horse, shot the head off the rattler, and then kicked the head far away—he knew that the head could still bite. Unfortunately, Riff was already spooked and Indy sure wasn't accustomed to close-up gunfire. The horses ran for the hills.

"The horses!" Lem yelled, cradling his left leg.

"Don't worry about the horses." Jim told him, crouching before his best friend. He removed his bandana and tied it tight above the fang marks the rattler had left in Lem's meaty calf. He removed Lem's scarf and tied it below the bite. Bayless worked like a seasoned medical man, swiftly making two cuts over the wound. He put his mouth to the bite mark, over Lem's objections, and began sucking-and-spitting the wound perfectly dry. He did not stop until the flesh was white, meaning he had gotten every drop.

Lem was crying. "Jimmy, God, Jimmy. I've killed you, my best friend. You'll die of that poison, brother."

"I won't, Lem. Now be still." He ordered. Over his partner's whimpers, he explained he could take the venom into his mouth without risk, so long as he had no wounds where the poison of the rattlesnake could get into his blood. An Indian squaw taught him that. She also showed him how to make a poultice for the wound site. Bayless would need a miniscule amount of foliage from the wild clematis (the vine was essentially poison), mixed with plantains—not the better known relative of the banana, but an overlooked weed that flourishes in nearly every state and territory in the country. Local white men called the weed 'snakegrass' or 'buckthorn', and it grew prolific in the Colorado foothills.

"I have to go find some plants for a poultice. You are going to sit still." Jim told him. Without waiting for his friend's reply, he dashed among the rocks and weeds in the low-lying foothills, searching for particular plant leaves.

Jim applied the hastily prepared poultice, and Lem told his friend he was certain no medical doctor could have done better. Jim said he would have liked to have Lem chew on the bruised root of some Black Cohosh, to combat the venom's violent side effects, but he did not know where to find the towering plant in this Territory. "Perhaps the doctor in the nearest town will have some", he offered, hopeful. "I am going to run to the nearest settlement and get us some help—and our horses." Jim patted his friend. "I mean it, Lemmy. Be still. I'll be back in less than an hour. Keep your gun beside you." He turned to remove his boots and socks.

"Jimmy, if I don't make it, I want you to take my belongings and do something with them. Don't bury anything with me, for crying out loud. I'm leaving it all to you, my brother."

Jim looked over his shoulder one more time, as his other sock dropped. "Don't talk like that, Lem. You're going to be fine. Have a little faith. And be still!" Jim Bayless discharged, fast as a hiccup. He followed in the same direction their horses ran.

He ran his heart out for five miles before a town came into sight. It was nestled between adolescent mountains, a main street plus a scramble of small cabins dotting the hillsides close to town...but not too close. Jim's heart was banging in his chest and his lungs were on fire. He had a pinch in one side that was beginning to give him real grief, but he kept on running.

The quaint little cabin was the furthest south of town, and so it was the first at which Bayless arrived. He struggled with thick hands to unlatch a gate to a picket fence that was just two-feet high. James was frustrated the owner would bother with such a silly hurdle. He stumbled up the porch steps, heaving, and weakly raised his hand to rap the door; that's when he saw it. It was a crude square of butcher's paper nailed to the door, and on it was written a single word: RUN.

"What the hell?" The sign momentarily stunned Jim. But then, as Vice Admiral Farragut said, 'damn the torpedoes!' He pounded on the door. The sound reverberated through an empty shack. The hair on Jim's head began to crawl backward on his scalp and the hair on his neck stood up straight. He decided to do as the sign was instructing. He ran.

Jim pushed aside the pain in his side and he continued his sprint into the town; he could not run easy, not when every second counted for poor Lem. Finally, his feet pounded the thin porch boards of a tiny home at the edge of the main street. It might also be a commercial business, Jim surmised, something with a woman's touch about it. There were curtains at the windows and carefully tended flower boxes beneath them. He was practically bent in half when he reached the door. When he pulled himself upright and raised his arm, he saw it. A smallish piece of torn paper tacked beneath an iron knocker. Written in red rouge or lipstick was the single word, "RUN".

"What in hell is going on here?" He yelled to the skies. He pounded on the entrance anyway, but the planks merely reverberated in the doorjamb. He turned around and surveyed the main street. It was odd; there were no people strolling, no animals left tethered to hitching posts, nothing. It was...quiet. *Good golly, somebody has to be alive in this town.* Jim tried to shake the confusion from his head. He sucked up his chest and once again ran slave to a cryptic note left on a strange door. He made up for the time he'd wasted. He worked his sprinter's legs faster than ever before—and blurred right past two living, breathing old men sitting outside the saloon. It took Jim twenty yards to come to a stop and circle back. When he did, those old men peered weird-peculiar at him, their jaws hanging wide.

It took nothing short of a Herculean effort for Bayless to push the four words out of his throat: "I need a doctor," he huffed at the men, not entirely sure he wasn't seeing a mirage.

One of the men removed his spectacles and wiped them clean. He placed them back on his nose. "How fast were you runnin', son?" He asked Jim.

Jim shook his head and looked around again. No, there did not seem to be anyone else living in this town. "Are you...ghosts?" Bayless asked them.

"Ghosts?" The other old timer laughed. "Don't bury me yet, son!" He laughed.

"I venture to say you was running near as fast as your horses, young fella. Which, by the by, are down the street at the furrier's."

Bayless looked from one man to the other. They looked just alike, right down to their long white beards. He shook his head clear one more time, and then screamed at the men. "Did you not hear me? I need a doctor, now!"

The bespectacled elder rose up from his chair, halfway. "Whoa, whoa. Settle down, son. There is no doctor in town, currently. Doc is at the run. He's visiting two towns over, in Harmony. That's where the traveling show went to, after they cleaned out our little town of Aria. Doc has it in his head he is goin' to get his money back."

"Doctors is supposed to be smart." The other senior observed.

"Well he ain't really a doctor anyhow, now is he?" He said to the other man. "Ignore my brother. But if you tell me what your trouble is, I might be able to help you. Doc never locks his office." The man offered.

On the way out to retrieve Lem, the two elders, Jake and Jess Durkin, retired sheep ranchers by trade, told Bayless why the town was empty. During the westward expansion that followed the Civil War, traveling medicine shows began to sprout up all about the country. They usually crashed small, bored western towns like Aria, offering gambling on competitions of all sorts, entertainment, and sometimes, albeit seldom, patent medical remedies. Actors, Shootists, Snake Oil Salesmen and Indians were often players in such troupes, the later performing war dances and other displays said to ward off evil; isolated frontier people are nothing if not superstitious.

The troupes usually pooled all their expenses and earnings, and then split the profits evenly among them, as gypsies tended to do; no one person was to be elevated above another. The problem was, none of the competitions for which they offered "friendly" gambling, were conducted on the up-and-up. They had their own "ringer" for every contest.

"One of their ilk arrived in Aria a few months ago. His name is Donny-something. He got work as a cowhand, and every minute he wasn't wrangling, he was curled up under a saloon table with a bottle, smelling like a moonshine factory." Jess said.

"'Course he weren't drinking at all, but we were none the wiser." Jake piped up.

"That's right, it was all an act. When this group of competitors came into town, they wanted volunteers for races of all sorts, which they were going to hold at the end of the week for prize money. Is was like a carnival atmosphere—ever been to a carnival, son?"

"Huh? No." Bayless was grateful for the old men's banter, but he wasn't really listening. He was worrying about his friend. Lem was bitten about an hour earlier. Bayless was sure he sucked out all the venom. Lem should be all right, so long as he sat still and didn't fall victim to any other dangers out here on the frontier.

"The fella, he called himself Doctor Benjamin, is a "promoter", he said. He trained runners and he liked to put his runners and his training abilities up against the common man of the West. He told us he could train any man we chose, and at the end of the week that man would run away with every race, pun intended. He was going to bet a thousand dollars of his own money on the man he trained for a hundred-yard sprint.

"I can tell ya, nobody I know in Aria was able to turn that down. 'Course you know how that story ended. We all bet against the drunk, trying for that $1,000 purse. But he wasn't a drunk, and he won every race, just like the promoter planned. The town lost a lot of money—and I mean, a lot." Jess growled.

As the wagon emerged from between two rock walls to the scattered lower foothills, the place where he left Lem, they saw what looked like two Indians molesting a dead man.

Jess Durkin hollered, "Ho!" at the natives and thrust a six-shooter in the air to show them he meant business.

The Ute foot soldiers froze in place. As the wagon rolled to a stop before them, one of the natives nervously looked to Bayless and said "talk turkey?"

Bayless shot an arm out and gestured to Jess Durkin that he knew these Indians; they were good Ute-Apache. He jumped down from the wagon and crouched on one knee next to Lem, who appeared to be lifeless. "Lem? Lemmy?" Jim shook the still man to no avail. He looked to the two Indians. Fear etched his face and grief filled his eyes. "He's not...is he? He can't be. He...I don't understand. Lem should have been all right. When I left him I thought he was all right." He shook Lem by his collar in a final sad attempt to rouse the young man, but he may as well have been shaking a bedroll. Jim's large hands dropped the fabric. He hung his head to cry. "Oh, Lem..."

One Indian lifted Lem's right hand and showed Bayless the tale.

"Chief said we should follow the red scarf, to make sure other Apache know you are a friend. After you run to the white man's town, we see Red Hair man look to find the head of his snake. And, see, he find it. He placed it in his hand, and the spirit of the snake bit him."

The punctures were telltale, as were the cuts over the bite. "Did he try to suck out the poison?" Jim asked the natives.

The Ute shook his head in whoa. "We make the cuts and draw out the poison, but we too late. Your friend, he jumps up and down and hollers; he shakes his snake bit hand—that is no good. We come fast to tell him, 'no move', but he is already sick. Now we are digging in ground for White Man burial." He explained what they were doing next to Lem's body.

Bayless was rendered mute. Lem was dead. Those were three words he never thought he would be saying. Dear God, why would he go after the snakehead Jim had purposefully kicked away? Why? He kept shaking his head. One of the Indians reached out and touched Jim's hand. "We dig now for friend." He offered.

Jim stood up and cleared his throat. "No. No, many thanks, my friends, for looking after Lem. But I best see to it he's buried some place his ma can find him."

The solemn natives nodded their understanding. Jim turned to face the Durkin brothers. "I reckon you have a cemetery in Aria, where Lem can rest?"

Chapter 5

Aria, Colorado

October 29, 1872

A quarter mile up from Main Street, James Bayless stood in shock and mourning with a Presbyterian Pastor, a gravedigger, and a local woman who agreed to sing "Amazing Grace" for Lem, acapella. At the moment, each one of them was staring at him.

He nodded at the pastor to begin.

> "In young manhood for Lemuel Hassen, he doth lay down in the quiet tomb. Delivered from the sunshine of life into the shades of death, he steps without tremor. His saint or unseen hand, upheld by the power of an unfathomable faith, has launched his frill craft upon, what would seem to his living brethren, a stormy sea. But for Lemuel it is a placid, glassy oceanic and the gilded decks of his glorious ship, whose waters are now eternity, knows not a storm.

> "Possessed of an imminently sorrowful mother and a heart-broken friend, James Bayless, to mourn his loss, the remains of this good Christian man shall be lowered into the narrow hose of the dead. There, in peaceful serenity, Lemuel will rest in undisturbed response, to remain until summoned by the voice of Him. And He will crown Lemuel Hassen with an imperishable immortality."

The digger began filling in the hole around the coffin. The preacher nodded at Bayless to say a few words over Lem.

Bayless cleared his throat and delivered a eulogy that he never would have believed possible. Lem was really gone. "Lem was only twenty-two years old. He was just a sophomore in the great seminary of experience, but fate must have taken advantage of that and conspired against him.

"He loved his ma, his horse and his friends. His favorite book was the Holy Bible. He thought the Sermon on the Mount was the ultimate message ever delivered, and he tried real hard to live by its teachings. He was sometimes naïve, often hilarious, and always a pal to man and beast.

"I think Lem is doing fine in the great hereafter. But if I had the chance to ask Lem five questions, I would ask him these:

1. Whatever happened to your dad, Lem?
2. Why did you and your ma move from Rocky Creek to Wheaton?
3. What was in the brown paper package delivered to the mercantile for you just before we left town?
4. Who sent the package?
5. Where do you buy those neat waist overalls?"

The late morning was strangely quiet, not a horse whinnied; not a bird chirped. Bayless searched the still terrain all around him and in a soft, shaking voice, said "Anyway, I loved him like a brother." He teetered to the edge of the grave and clumsily dropped a handful of loamy soil atop the wooden casket. "What am I going to tell your mother, Lem?" He said to the coffin. He smeared a tear and walked away; down the hill, down the main street, and into the saloon. A pitchy soprano lilted on the breeze. James Bayless wasn't normally a drinker, but he would be on that day.

By noontime, every denizen of Aria knew who the stranger hitting it hard in the saloon was. They knew his name was Bayless, and they knew he was real fast. All they really needed to know now was if he was willing to run for them. Jim sat in the center of the bar facing racks of glasses against a stained mirror. Tears streamed down his face unfettered. He appeared motionless, save for the repetition of glass to lips. Jess Durkin approached and stood silently on one side of Bayless. His brother arrived to flank his other side.

"Don't have a worry, but those two odd, old fellas in the mirror are staring at us." Jake Durkin tried for a bit of lightheartedness. James just stared into the mirror at the men.

Jess spoke up. "Terrible day. It is a black, terrible, terrible day. I am awfully sorry about your friend, Bayless." Jessie told him.

"Thank you," Jim managed.

"Me, too." Jake said.

"Thank you."

"Barkeep, we'll share a salute to the fella's friend, and get Bayless here another one too." Jessie said. The bartender lined up three shots. The Durkin brothers both raised a glass. Bayless silently imitated them. "To Lem." Jessie Durkin toasted.

"To Lem," the other two repeated.

After a minute passed in hushed silence, Jessie said, "We know you have to return to Missouri with money. We can't have you losing your girl, too. We have a proposition."

Jim turned on his stool and stared at Jess.

"Run for us. Be our 'ringer' in the foot races over in Harmony. Help the town get its money back, and we'll split it with you."

Jim shook his head. "I'm sorry, men, but I need a lot of money. I need a few thousand dollars. I need to dig for gold, and I guess I'm going to be doing it alone."

"I'm saying, half, Bayless. We'll split it with you. It ain't hay feed, young man. That traveling troupe took us for more than $22,000."

Jessie Durkin bent down and rubbed a cramp from Bayless' left foot. He had to tuck his beard inside his shirt so it didn't tickle his runner's leg. "How's that? How are you feeling today, overall?

"That's good. I'm fine. My feet are not used to being bound in shoes. That's why I keep getting Charlie-horses." James told him.

"Well that's no good, James. If you're faster in bare feet, then from here on I want you practicing barefoot. And for certain, I want you to run your race barefoot. But like everything else about you, Bayless, I want the bare feet to be a surprise.

"We'll keep leaving before daybreak to head out here to the canyon—ain't anyone but Indians out here. You'll get your training in, and then you can put your running shoes on for the ride back to town. They won't be expecting a barefoot runner who's not even Indian, and that means they cannot hinder your feet." He answered.

"Hinder my feet? I don't understand." Jim pushed himself up and began jumping jacks.

"The night before the race in Aria, someone stole the shoes of the fastest racers. Other shoes were found later to have had their soles replaced by a layer of lead, making them much, much heavier. Trust me, they will try to sabotage your running shoes, Bayless, because they will think you need them."

"Ah. Won't they be surprised?" Bayless dripped with sarcasm. "I hate cheaters," he added.

"That's good, son. You keep that pent up until the race and then let it go. You're going to need it. Their fella is originally from Scotland, and he is *fast*. They say he's won lots of races across the sea."

"I'll be faster." Jim stated. He knew he would be faster, because he had to be. He would return to Wheaton, to Maggie, with more than enough gold to win her hand, or he would die trying.

The troupe didn't know anything about Bayless, and they seemed completely unconcerned with him and his entry in the racing competition. That was probably because they never saw Bayless training for a race. As a result, the troupe's "ringer", Donny by name, loafed in confidence. In lieu of training, Donny preferred instead to eat T-bone steaks for lunch, followed with plenty of red wine, followed by a long nap. At night, Donny was back in the saloon playing cards until late. He usually took a woman to his room afterward.

Bayless, like Donny, enjoyed a good steak or half-chicken with potatoes and gravy for his supper. But in direct contradiction, Bayless went to bed early and rose early—alone. Furthermore, he had Jessie and Jake for his trainers. The brothers drove him each day to a red-dirt canyon where the earth was soft and fairly level. Bayless would run 120-yard dashes in training for the 100-yard, building his endurance. He then did some stretches, and some sprints up the soft dirt hillsides of the canyon to improve his stamina. Bayless did this for about an hour, baffling the Ute Apache assigned to look out for him. He kept the red sash in clear view, tied to the halter of the lead ox. When the men and their wagon returned to town, Bayless wore the red sash tied about his middle, and extremely light-weight, oil grain running slippers on his feet, just in case anyone was paying attention. Most folks were just beginning to rise-and-shine.

Doctor Benjamin was a tall man with a ruddy complexion and a shock of grey hair at his temples. The rest of his nondescript head was generously covered with wavy dark brown hair, perhaps with a nick of red to it. Benjamin was paying attention to Bayless. He felt someone should. No one seemed to know anything about the man, and no one had seen him train. Ordinarily Benjamin wouldn't have a worry, but Bayless was a wild card—a wild card with very long legs and a runner's air about him; Benjamin knew a runner when he saw one. "Time for you to shape up, Donny. You have been lounging easy for too long. Time to start running."

"Lounging easy? Is that what they call breathing three weeks of dust riding behind a herd of bull's asses, playing like a drunken cowpoke who you could learn to race? Because that's what I've been doing to play my part. I deserve some nights off. Lounging easy, indeed." Donny bristled.

"Now you listen up, Donny-boy. You need to quit your late nights, starting now. You need to get nine hours of sleep each night over the next few days, and it wouldn't hurt you to stretch out those racing legs, is what I'm saying."

Donny looked at Benjamin and yawned. "What? You're worried about that guy what run into town a few days ago?"

"Worried? No. Concerned, yes. He has legs longer than the Missouri River. Beyond those stems of his he is an unknown, and therefore unpredictable. That is cause for concern when there is already nearly $30,000 of our money booking bets for and against him. I have to place that much, in money or in metal, in the hands of the Events Commissioner before any racing starts. "

That got Donny's attention. "I didn't know we did that. Do we always do that?"

Benjamin was exasperated with their young runner, his deceased brother's only child. Before Doc had become Custodian for Donny Benjamin, who was just a teen at the time, Doctor Benjamin had been a runner, himself—a trained 'Fast Man'. Even at forty-four years of age, he still entered and won plenty of races. But one day, and he hoped that day came soon, he wanted to retire from racing altogether and make his living training runners and promoting competitions, both here in the untapped American West, and maybe over the seas.

These little western towns were perfect for sharpening his nephew's teeth. Frontier people were a rag tag mix of miner, farmer, merchant and cow-buster. In commonality, they were a fairly trusting bunch of God-fearing folks. But if Donny didn't start taking his role more serious, he could one day find himself up against a genuinely faster man…and he could lose. "If we want to book bets, we do. Which brings me back to, 'get off your duff and start training'. Furthermore, you will have your dinner meal at a reasonable hour, followed by a *short* nap and a light supper, before an early bedtime. I want you in sound shape before I put that much money on your nose."

Donny gave a nasty snort that doubled for a laugh. "I don't think that's goin' to happen, Unc."

A cuff on the ear came out of nowhere and landed the young man on the floor. "I do. And don't ever call me that." He grabbed his nephew by his other ear and pulled him to his feet, amid high-pitched pleas to let go. Next thing Donny knew, he was behind the saloon running sprints against himself, with an increasingly harsh thumping in his head courtesy his drinking of the night before.

"Thank you for seeing me, Pastor Morris." Silas Biggs looked mighty uncomfortable as his eyes surveyed the small church. He cowed as though he expected a great hand to descend from the cathedral ceiling at any moment and smack him.

"Of course, Silas. Any time you need to talk, we are here for you."

"We?" Silas questioned.

"The Lord and myself, Silas. But most especially when a man's heart is at risk. Now, who is this man, and how can I help him?"

49

"It's me, Pastor. It's my heart. I'm hesitating to tell you why because…" his eyes darted toward the ceiling as though expecting a blow. "It's because I know you ain't gonna like my answer."

"I am not here to judge you, Silas." Daniel Morris said simply.

Biggs cleared his throat. "I'll tell you what, Pastor. I've been feeling a little…it's been four years since that filthy squaw left me—"

"No-no." Morris shook his head at Silas.

"Sorry, Pastor. I shouldn't lie in a house of God. I know she wasn't filthy, and she was only half Cherokee."

Pastor Morris raised his eyebrows at the convoluted apology, his eyes wide, but Biggs did not seem to take note. "She was a long-sick woman, Silas. She left her life, not you, and not your son. Try to have pity for her."

"Pity? You and the Lord ain't angry with her? Ain't it a sin to take your own life? I was told it was. You know she didn't take that dose of Rough on Rats by accident. Says right on the can fatality will result in just a few hours, no matter the doctor in Cassville tried every effort to save her life."

"If I remember her story correct, her mother delivered her into this world, and Barry County in particular, back in '39, fresh off the Trail of Tears. She was forced to walk that long, hard journey from Tennessee to Oklahoma all throughout her pregnancy. The baby was born sickly."

"So." Silas replied.

"So, Silas, her mother might have been a tough little knot, but your wife wasn't. She had been in ill health for a long, long time. I'm not saying it is her right to judge and conclude her own life. I am saying she was ill a long time and she became despondent. Then she was despondent for a long time, and arguably not even herself after a spell. She made up her mind to end her life of misery, not her marriage. No other cause should be assigned. You need to find it in your heart to forgive her, Silas."

Biggs grumbled a barely discernible, "I guess." He rose from the hard wooden chair and nervously paced before the pastor's desk. "My point is I have been yearning for a woman's touch. That cabin I share with my half-wit son, it's too…I'm starting to feel lonesome." He searched the face of the pastor for signs of roadblocks, but saw none. Morris, to his credit, was perfectly composed. "For the past few months I've been leading my son, like I would lead a horse to water, toward the prettiest, smartest, highest-quality woman in all the county. I've been prodding him toward a marrying mindset, and talking up this particular woman's obvious attributes, but also her less obvious qualities, such as kindness, intelligence and spirituality. Pastor, that boy is turned twenty years old already, and he still don't even have a passing interest in the girl—or any girl. It's maddening, I can tell ya."

Morris blinked. "Are you trying to say your boy is of doubtful gender?"

"What's that?" Biggs asked.

"Does he prefer the company of his own sex greater than that of a female?"

Morris stopped in his tracks. "What? No! God, no." He protested, shaking his head. "My son is not...look, here's the thing, Pastor. Talking this woman up for a spell, and knowing that my son ain't the least bit interested for himself, I sort of...I have become..." He glanced quickly at the Pastor, then away. "I have, myself, become smitten with this female. I would like to marry her for my own self and I have my son's blessing."

Pastor Morris felt sympathy for the big man before him. The Lord had been good to Biggs in terms of personal wealth, but life had not been especially generous or kind otherwise. Morris knew rumors circulated Wheaton about the man's character, or lack thereof, but he had never been one to put much stock in tongue wagging. When it came to gossip, it took him slow years to learn, even the best of the Lord's herd tended to exaggerate. Perhaps Biggs was gruff because he was hurting and lonely.

"And how is it I can be of help to you, Silas?" Morris asked.

"You can give me permission, Pastor."

"You don't need my permission, Silas. Your first wife died and you are free to remarry. All you need to do is sign a few papers up at Cassville for a marriage license."

"Aw hell, I'm just gonna say it, flat out. I want to marry your daughter, Preacher." Silas said, finally removing his big white hat.

Her hands rushed to protect her middle and hold down her breakfast. She paced the little cabin, frantic. "Father, how could you even entertain such an idea? Silas Biggs? He is, I mean, you must admit he's a little hard on the eyes. And I know you don't cater to gossip, but Silas is said to be just as ugly on the inside. Great gravy, father, he is even older than you are. The whole idea...is revolting."

"Margaret Ellen—"

"No. I won't do it, father. I will not see him. You know I love Jim Bayless. The man is, right now, risking his life on a wild frontier, because you would not give him your blessing to marry me. 'Return from Colorado with gold enough for a proper dowry and you may have her hand' you said. Are you now giving him no time to do so?"

Morris considered his daughter. He loved her independent streak. He thought it a good quality for a modern woman to possess and he had encouraged it in her as she grew. But perhaps he should have listened to the wisdom of more experienced parents, and beat some of it back out of her. "I gave my permission for Silas to call on you. I did not promise him your hand. Silas Biggs is mature, I know. But, he is also quite stable, financially sound, and smitten with you, dear, smitten indeed. As for the ugliness, I believe it is merely skin-deep. I saw some light in that soul of his. I know my daughter is neither superficial, nor a gossip. Therefore I found no harm in letting him come calling. The rest is up to you, Margaret Ellen. And that is precisely what I told Mr. Silas Biggs." He gave his daughter a patient smile.

"I'm going to be sick." Maggie announced, running from the room.

Chapter 6

Harmony, Colorado

October 31, 1872

Kenneth Benjamin held an advanced degree in mathematics from London University. He had always displayed a natural keenness with numbers, but the subject bored him overall. That was until he discovered gambling and the art of running. The two interests complimented each other, and had made Benjamin a wealthy man. When the aging Doc started feeling the races he ran on the following day, he decided it a good time to train his replacement, Donny. The boy was naturally fast but he lacked discipline. Benjamin was able to administer enough of the rod to get Donny-boy this far, but the lad was far from restrained.

Benjamin knew odds like nobody's business, and the odds were that someone would come along and trounce Donny. Doc Benjamin wondered if that scenario were about to play out in Harmony, with over $30,000 at risk. *Is James Bayless that Fast Man?* He wondered. If he turned out to be, Benjamin would be ruined.

"We need to shore up our odds for tomorrow. I am only concerned about one race and a single runner, that Bayless fellow. He's an unknown." Benjamin explained. An unknown variable had the potential to demolish Benjamin's odds.

"What do you need?" asked the troupe member who sold herbal remedies for ailments like winter fever, arthritis, and snakebites, and to such cures as placebos. Frontier folks often referred to such men as "Snake-Oil Salesmen". But a handful of Hank's blends, the ones he learned from Native Americans, could actually score positive results.

"Tonight when he goes to sleep, I want you to take his running shoes. I want you to rip out the leather stitching that secures the vamp to the sole, and then stitch it back up with common cotton thread, black of course, so that it goes unnoticed. The shoes won't last three strides before the sole splits away and folds back on itself."

"He's gonna take one hell of a fall. Might even ruin him from racing, altogether." Hank mused.

"I admit that possibility bothers me a little, but since when do you care?"

"I don't, really." Hank blew a smoke ring in the air with his cigar.

"You know I don't want to mangle Bayless, but I have to get more odds in our favor. This is a man who may have the potential to run away with our hard-earned gold, Hank—every bit of it."

The troupe medicine man laughed. "I don't care if he wins a race, or not. He's not ever going to run away with our money. We've been dancing, singing and acting for podunks all summer and fall for that gold. It was hard work and we earned it. The races at the end of the week, those are just the frosting. That money is ours."

"Here we are. It's racing day and believe you me, those coffers in the Commission tent are full." Jess Durkin declared.

"Doctor Benjamin and his merry band of charlatans think the money is rightfully theirs. " Jake added.

"Yes," Jessie agreed. "They make their living pulling swindles on towns like Aria and Harmony. We know they're just a bunch of actors with maybe one good Fast Man, and we know they think our fortunes are their due, for the entertainment they provide." Jess Durkin explained.

"They would be wrong." Bayless answered simply.

Jess and his brother exchanged glances. "So, you are feeling good, then? You're feeling strong, Jim? Can you take that Donny fella? No blustering, now."

"I can take him," Jim answered with finality.

"Good." Jess said. "Then this is how it's going to go down tomorrow: We'll have your horse and gear ready to ride, just a half-mile northeast of town. The Games Commission tent is just beyond your race's finish line. They will have your winnings split into two bags, half for you and half for us. After you cross the finish line, you'll keep running to that tent, you'll grab a money bag and you'll just keep on running until you reach your horse. You'll catch that train at Tarn City well before the men who are sure to follow you, and you'll be home free."

"Except I am not getting on that train."

"You have to," Jake exclaimed. "You have to know, them troupe fellas are gonna come for that prize money. The only thing harder than winning the purse will be getting it back to Missouri. We don't really know these charlatans, Bayless. They could be the killing sorts."

"Anybody is the killing sort for that kind of money. You'll need to get out of Harmony, fast." Jess agreed.

"They're going to assume I am on that train and I imagine they will aim to get someone on it, too. If any of them were to board, Indy and I would be captives. I know it will be a danger to run across the Kansas Territory, but I can do it on foot. They'll never catch me. Plus, I'll have a couple of friends looking out for me." Bayless looked down at the red silk tied at his middle and memories of Lem assaulted him. The sash made him look a little like a pirate, but he didn't care. James called it his "good luck scarf".

Jess patted their young racer on the back. "I don't even think I'll need to worry for you, son. You'll make it back to Missouri, back to your Maggie. I know you will. Just run, Bayless. Run like you've never run before."

The day's competitions began with greased pig contests, steeplechases and harness racing. Stores on the main thoroughfare found their street crowded with wagons and people arriving to watch the events. Farmers' wives in homemade dresses tried to finish their shopping and trading amid boardwalks already gridlocked with enthusiasts of the morning's competitions. They hauled their groceries through the crowds, often chasing and yelling at younger children who were loose and scampering through the multitudes.

Marathon runners left at daybreak, and some folks in wagons followed their progress. The pigeon races intrigued Jake. He couldn't figure how someone could choose a bird and know it would fly fast and true, but one of the actor fellas who ran the contest seemed to pick the right bird every time.

Jessie promised his brother that sure as a bull is in the spring, the charlatans must have "fixed" the pigeon races somehow. He aimed to find out about it. He crept up behind the actor and watched the man's hands as he held the next pigeon to challenge his. Just before the hands let the bird fly, He saw the actor palm a doornail and blind the poor thing in one eye. The challenging bird could not fly straight, so the actor's bird won again. Jessie blew the whistle.

He grabbed the smaller man by the lapel of his wrinkled shirt and dragged him into the middle of the action in the street. Farmers in Tuf-Nut bib overalls halted loading a transport wagon with cattle feed, chicken feed and gallons of bug spray for the livestock. Other men who already finished with their town business and were gathered here-and-there in small groups, ceased their smoking and quit their talk about the weather and the price of hay and cows.

"I can't abide cruelty to critters, folks. This fella has a doornail up his grip and he has just blinded his last pigeon," Jessie fairly hollered. "And you will return the money you took from these nice folks by cheating with those blinded birds." He shook the man before releasing his collar.

Doctor Benjamin strolled into the mix and asked of his colleague, "Is this true? You *permanently* blinded some pigeons to ensure your wins?" He tisk-tisk'd and waved his finger in front of the man. To the others gathering around, he promised, "We do not abide such cruelty either, good people of Harmony. Goodness, no. We are here to spread good health and good cheer—and perhaps even a bit of good wealth. I give you my word and solemn promise that Reuben here will never permanently blind another bird, ever again."

The denizens of Harmony had chosen their elected sheriff to act as Game Commissioner. He began to dole back to some folks the wagers they had made on the blinded birds. The remaining gatherers vacated the street so the games could continue. No one noticed when Benjamin nodded at another actor troupe member who was loitering near the pigeon cages. The man nodded back and exposed a small bottle filled with tobacco juice. He made his way over to Reuben, the bird-blinder. Before long, the townsfolk were once again emptying their pockets on crooked-flying pigeons.

"Please, come in, Silas. I assume from the beautiful flowers that you have come calling for Maggie?" The preacher led the way to their tiny sitting area. "I'll fetch Margaret for you." He headed down a short hall.

Maggie still didn't have her shoes on when she heard her father with Silas, at the front door—the only door. Ah, but she had a window, didn't she? She tried mightily to lift the wood framed glass on its pulley, but it was stuck. Her father knocked on the door.

When his knock was met with silence and he knew his daughter was inside, he wondered if she might be napping. He gingerly opened the door. It squeaked, but no matter. Maggie was sitting on the end of her bed facing him. "You have a guest, Margaret. Come out and say a polite hello, like you've been raised right."

"I do not want to see Silas Biggs. He makes my skin crawl. Just tell him I am napping and not feeling well."

"Are you asking me to lie for you?" Her father asked, incredulous.

Maggie sighed and met her father's eyes. "No. I don't want you to lie for me. It's mostly true, though, father. Whenever I think of him I do feel nauseated."

"Margaret, please lower your voice. I will let him know you will be joining him shortly. So, please do." Preacher Morris whispered.

Maggie racked her brains trying to think of a way out of this "courtship" her father had arranged. Perhaps she could make Silas Biggs less interested in her. She never wore makeup, but she could make herself much less attractive by chopping off her hair. Jim, however, loved her coal-black hair.

She had an idea she was certain would work, if she could find the nerve to go through with it. She chewed her lower lip for a moment and then looked at herself in the mirror. "I will visit with Silas Biggs, providing it is just a visit and he does not try anything. But I know what to do, should he try to force this marriage idea...or me." She told her reflection. She rose and smoothed her dress, smiled graciously and left her room. The short hallway had never seemed so long. There at the end of it an old man sat holding a bouquet.

"Mr. Biggs, this is a surprise. Are those for me?" she nodded at the flowers. He nodded at her and silently handed them over.

'It's Silas, if you please. Silas." He told her before she left the room.

Preacher Morris tried to give Silas some company while his daughter searched for a vase. She had been searching for a spell. "Do you need some assistance?" Her father called to her.

"No, father". She put down the spoon she had been using to randomly clang, clink and rummage among a pretty sparse stock of kitchen and household items. She picked up her only vase and filled it half full with water. She cut the ends off the flowers and stuffed them inside the vase. She untied the ribbon and let the flowers go. They were beautiful. She retied the yellow ribbon about the top of the vase and carried the arrangement into the other room. She set the vase upon a table made of two crates and two planks of wood and declared she had never seen anything so beautiful. She meant it. "Thank you…Silas." She said quietly.

He patted the small sofa next to him. Maggie looked nervously to her father.

"Maggie, maybe you could set out some of that elk sausage and homemade bread for our guest." He turned to Biggs. "If you have not tasted it, Silas, it is a taste worth remembering." The preacher told him.

"I would rather have Maggie come sit next to me." He replied.

Maggie walked slowly, and when she sat, she squeezed herself as close as possible against the armrest of the sofa, giving her less than an inch of daylight between them. He smelled of tobacco and steer manure. She noticed, with brow furrowed, Silas had not bothered to remove his dirty boots before tracking that manure all through her clean house. Suddenly Silas readjusted in his seat and now he was squeezed against her. Her eyes jumped to her father in near panic, but he seemed to know not what to do about the matter. Then, Silas placed his arm around her and drew her into his armpit.

"I thought we would have a bit of steak in town, then perhaps take a walk in the full-moon light. What do you say, Mags?" Silas breathed on her.

Maggie's head swam. She was suddenly dizzy and the cloying smell of sweet tobacco and cow-patties was making her stomach flip. She felt caged...claustrophobic. "Father!" She jumped to her feet, startling all present. "I'm pregnant." She blurted. She turned to a gape-mouthed Silas Biggs and told him, "I am sorry to have wasted your time, Mr. Biggs, but I am with another man's child, a man I am engaged to be married to, mind you, and nonetheless I cannot be courted."

"Margaret Ellen...you are with child?" Her father found his voice. She nodded, unable to meet his eyes.

Silas took the whole scene in and had to wonder how much of it was true. Her father seemed to buy the story so perhaps he left the young couple unchaperoned on occasion. Biggs wasn't sure he believed it, but no matter. Time would certainly tell. He stood and placed his hat on his head.

"Preacher Morris, your daughter's beloved has embarked upon a dangerous mission, and who knows if he may ever return." He paused when he heard Maggie catch her voice. He turned to her. "It is a possibility we, as prudent adults, must at least deliberate. Now, if she wasn't pregnant, she might wait for his return until her bones turned to dust. But she is, and that pregnancy will begin to show, soon enough. How long?" He asked.

"A few weeks." She said simply. She mustered her nerve and stared down her father. "James Bayless will return to me. I know it."

"I would say in December, she's going to have to let out clothing. The pregnancy could show. Some do at two months. That could become an embarrassment for a preacher, no?" Silas asked Morris.

Daniel Morris ignored his guest. "Maggie…Maggie…what will you do if Bayless gets himself killed along the way there or on his way back? We have no relatives to send you to, no explaining a pregnancy without a husband. I am afraid you have thoroughly mixed up your life, young lady. I honestly do not know what to do about you." The preacher said. He looked so sad Maggie wanted to cry.

"James Bayless will come back to me, I know he will!" In a moment of uncharacteristic frustration and anger, she raised her voice.

As if she had said nothing at all, Biggs answered his own question. "Yes, an embarrassment, to be sure. I might make a suggestion, if you've an ear, preacher." Biggs waited for a go-ahead. He received a blank look, which he took as a pass to go on. "Now, mind you, I don't need a wife the whole town is going to gossip about—I had one of those. So my offer's good only until she starts showing, or the calendar flips to December 1, whichever occurs first. If Bayless don't return by that date, I will marry Maggie and call the baby mine. Your daughter and baby will be well taken care of, preacher. And no one will be the wiser if she happens to have her baby a month early; it happens. You can rest easy."

Preacher Morris looked at his daughter. He rose a bit unsteady and shook Biggs' hand. Maggie could not believe what she was hearing and seeing. She felt far removed, as if she was watching the events unfold from someone else's eyes. When she finally got hold of herself she squeaked, "what? Nooo." Then holding her stomach and her mouth, she ran from the room.

"She has the nausea," Morris explained to Silas.

"Ah, that. Poor girl. Tell her I do hope this stage goes quickly for her." He said, finding his own way to the door. "December 1, then. We shook on it. Thank you, preacher." He closed the door behind him.

Chapter 7

Harmony, Colorado

October 31, 1872

Indy seemed nervous standing at the side of the Commission tent. She stamped her feet as Jake Durkin tied the last of Jim' possessions to her rump and made ready to ride the mare just outside of town, where Bayless would meet them. She was a pretty sorrel, over fifteen hands high. She had a full belly and fleshy haunches that helped sustain her over long trips, and she easily handled the weight of Bayless' short mail rides.

Kenneth Benjamin watched Bayless as he stretched his body out wearing the sabotaged running shoes. The promoter searched out the actor he'd charged with "fixing" Bayless' running shoes and raised his eyebrows at him. The actor smiled and nodded in reply. Finally, Benjamin allowed himself to relax. He even broke out a grand smile to wear, his first in days. The unknown variable had been nullified.

The Sheriff's deputy made his way to the far side of the thoroughfare near the starting line. This told the sprinters their race was up, and all nine of the men who entered the competition made their way to the line. Jessie whispered to Bayless, telling him Jake had already ridden Indy to the outskirts of town and was waiting for him.

"Good luck and God love ya, Bayless. Give it everything you've got, including the hair and the holler, for Maggie and for all of us. No matter what happens, son, you be sure to send us a note and let us know you made it back to Missouri safe. All-righty?" Jess smacked James on the back.

Every runner was pulling final stretches and lunges to loosen their legs. The deputy, with pistol hand in the air, called the runners to their mark. James lined himself up in the middle of the pack, ripped off the shoes that Doc Benjamin's man had so carefully sabotaged, and tossed them over to Jessie.

Benjamin saw this and was nonplussed. "What? He's going to run barefoot?" He exclaimed.

Thanks to Kenneth Benjamin, all eyes were on Bayless when the pistol fired.

Something told Griselda Hassen to peek—just a peek, mind you, at the package Lem picked up at the mercantile post office the day before he left town. Zelda wasn't of usual the nosing around type of woman. Truth-be-told, she neither received nor enjoyed surprises. But the mystery of Lem's delivered parcel had invaded her dreams of the night before. At breakfast, the secret gnawed on her, until by noontime, she felt she would die if she didn't find out about that package. Zelda had made up her uneasy mind. She crept inside her son's tidy sleeping area and she pulled the brown-papered bundle from beneath his sagging mattress. She made a mental note to tighten those bed-straps and air out that mattress before her cherished son returned home.

She placed the bundle atop the bed. The package had already been opened and inspected by her son, apparently. A pair of waist overalls was folded atop another box. The pants were far too long to be for Lemuel, and she surmised her son had ordered them for long-legged Jim Bayless, when first he agreed to go prospecting with Lem. Her son had no way of knowing about this trip all of those weeks ago when the pants were ordered from San Francisco. How fortunate they arrived in time, and how like her Lem to forget to pack them for the trip, she smiled to herself.

Zelda set the pants aside and opened a reinforced box. She stared at the contents a good while before her shaking hand could lift the note card with Lem's familiar scrawl across it. "For Ma, on her birthday" the front of the card read. Something about her dream the night before, something she couldn't recall in the morning, was warning her away, but Zelda persisted. *Silly superstitious old woman*, she scolded herself. She opened it with ginger-fingertips and her eyes scanned the note card while her brain screamed at her that she shouldn't have snooped.

Have the happiest of birthdays, Ma. I don't want you to be lonely when I'm gone. I know the only reason you did not join the Ladies' Bridge Group for their afternoon tea and cards, is because you don't own a tea set...or cards. I fixed that. Now go play, and have fun! Your loving son, Lem

Something cold and oily scurried through the cabin and up Griselda Hassen's leg. It crawled up her spine and reached horrible gnarled talons over her bony shoulders to grip her heart and squeeze it. Griselda Hassen grabbed at her heart and fainted.

The races were being run according to English Pedestrianism Rules: two starting-commands and then the gun. Nine men lined up for the 100-yard sprint, but there were only three men to watch; a Native American from Bayless' neck of the woods who had already won the mile-run, Donny the "ringer", on whose head Doctor Benjamin placed his fortune, and the latecomer, Bayless. It seemed the folks were most curious about the latecomer.

"On your mark," the deputy yelled. Eight men placed one foot on the line and their arms in pumping mode. Bayless amazed the crowd once again, and rattled his fellow racers as well, when he practically took a knee, the ball of his right foot in front of his left and on the line, along with spread fingers of both his hands. The deputy appeared nonplussed; he looked to the sheriff. The sheriff stood at the finish line to ensure the two men holding the length of knotted white sheets didn't pull any funny business, like trying to move the finish line. The sheriff shrugged. There were no rules that said you had to start your race standing upright.

"Get set," the deputy hollered. Bayless raised his back end slightly and the crowd clamored some more. Spectators could see his fingers had turned white with the pressure the runner was placing on them.

BANG. Bayless immediately emerged from the pack of runners in the middle of the course, like he was shot out of a canon. At twenty yards, Donny, on the inside, was only a half-stride behind Bayless. The Indian was running on the outside of the pack. By forty yards, he had clearly fallen into third place. The spectators at the sides of the track could see no daylight between Bayless and Donny, but Benjamin was worried. Bayless could run. In fact, Bayless might be the fastest untrained runner he'd ever seen, and the man was running in bare feet. He watched as Bayless' long legs stretched and reached for every stride with the ball of his feet; he was a natural. At sixty yards, the Indian's feet were slapping the hard dirt, heel first—a sure sign he was already wearying from trying to catch the front-runners.

Bayless could hear his blood pulsing in his ears, and from much further away the raucous cheers of the crowd. At eighty yards, a slightly sweaty and fiery sensation broke out about his face and neck but his breathing was clean and even.

Donny Benjamin could feel his own breathing ravaging his throat, and his piston-pumping legs were tiring. Doc Benjamin could see Donny was fatigued, and suddenly there was a crack of daylight between the runners. "Thrash him, Donny! Pour it on now!" Benjamin yelled at his protégé. Donny turned his head sideways to see if he was even with Bayless, and that was telltale. The crowd was all a frenzy and rooting for the stranger, Bayless.

Jim took strength from Doc Benjamin's urgings to his own runner to catch up to him—*that must mean I am in the lead, no need to go looking.* Jim surmised. That spurred him to dig down and find a surging strength, like a subterranean river rolling through his deep. He sped forward, nearly flying the last ten yards of the race, his chest and head stretched forward toward the taut bed-sheet finish line. *I've got this Maggie!* Bayless' body, mind and soul joined together to shout at the heavens. He toppled through the sheets a full stride ahead of the ringer, who threw himself at the finish line only to topple and brutally smack the ground just shy of it.

Most eyes were on the fallen runner. But to the fun and amazement of a handful of spectators still watching the latecomer who'd won the race, Bayless caught his balance and kept right on running, all the way to the Commission tent. "He is sure in a hurry to collect his winnings" someone joked. But even those few watchers did not see Bayless scoop up a prepared bag of gold from the Game Commissioner and continue running beyond the tent, beyond Main Street, and finally beyond Harmony. The first, and arguably most difficult part of Bayless' and the Durkins' plan, had gone off without a hitch.

If it was commotion among the spectators, it was nothing short of melee between the traveling troupe and Benjamin's bookmakers, who had been milling through the crowds. They all made their way to Benjamin, and they all wanted an answer to the same questions: How much are they going to have to pay out to the town of Harmony? Did they just lose all of their money by betting everything on the ringer?

"Calm down, let us have some calm, please. I know a lot of late money was put down on Bayless to win and, yes, we had our peckers pulled out pretty far on this. But look at whom you are talking to." He laughed, albeit a bit uneasy. "Of course I am not going to allow those tricksters to run off with all our profits. Just before the race started, I heard that sheep rancher from Aria holler to Bayless. He said to send them a note when he made it back to Missouri. Gentlemen, Mr. Bayless may make it to his home in Missouri, but I can promise you our money will not be going with him. We will follow him when he leaves town and when we have him to ourselves, we will retrieve our money. Consider the matter taken care of." He promised

Reverend Richardson paid a visit to Maggie Morris while she worked with her rabbits. He purchased a plump one for his Sunday dinner and arranged to have it transferred to the butcher in town. Then he got down to the other business he had come for.

"I don't know if you heard, but a member of my flock, Griselda Hassen, Lemuel's mother, has suffered a heart spell. I have church ladies taking turns caring for Zelda until she can get back on her feet; I was hoping I might also enlist your assistance. I know you are friendly with Lemuel."

"Of course, Reverend Richardson. Anything I can do to help. When did this happen?" Maggie asked.

Richardson took one of Maggie's hands in his and thanked her. "She was found yesterday afternoon, when she failed to make her Bible Study group. Apparently Griselda's heart suffered a severe spasm after she was struck by the idea that her son would not be returning home to her. She believes Lemuel is dead, and I am afraid I have had no luck in swaying her from the idea."

Maggie's normally caramel complexion turned white as parchment at the news. She pulled her hand back and busied herself with the rabbits, holding back tears.

"Oh, my dear, I have gone and upset you. I did not mean for--"

"Why does Mrs. Hassen think Lem is...gone?" Maggie asked. *And what about Jim?*

"It had to do with a dream she had, which she cannot remember, poor little bird. And then she found a package or gift for her that her son had stashed under his bed, and whatever was inside that box gave her quite a fright. I must admit, I do not understand it. All she will say is she wants her son with her, not tea with the ladies. She has done a host of crying, I'll say, and even seems to have aged some overnight, what with wringing herself dry.

"She's so positive?" Maggie murmured softly.

"Perhaps you could speak with her, Margaret? We need someone to watch her from noontime to dinner, when Mrs. Peabody is finished with her quilting group."

Maggie genuinely felt ill. Griselda Hassen is believed to have a touch of insight, and she is so certain her son is gone. What about Jim? Her mind kept asking over and over. "Yes, of course, Reverend Richardson. I will talk with Mrs. Hassen, and I will bring a luncheon with me."

The Reverend breathed with relief. "I thank you kindly, my dear. I was so hoping to be able to count on you."

Maggie tapped on the front door and entered. "Hello, Mrs. Hassen. It's Maggie Morris. I have brought some lunch with me." She called out. She pressed further into the small cabin and found bedridden Griselda in a small room off the kitchen. A coarse blanket hanging over the doorway separated it. The blanket had been cast aside and tacked to the wall.

"Margaret," Griselda almost whispered. She gave the young girl a weak smile.

Maggie rushed to her bedside and held the woman's hand. "I was so sorry to hear of your illness. How are you feeling today, Mrs. Hassen?"

Griselda smiled sadly at her. "I don't think I will ever feel right again, Margaret. Lem is gone. I don't know how, but I know it." Her eyes spilled over. Maggie's joined in.

"Could it be you're just homesick for your son, Mrs. Hassen? Maybe that's the cause of your heartache." Maggie told her, hoping against hope that it wasn't true.

That time, Griselda Hassen reached and patted the back of Maggie's hand in a comforting manner. "There are just some things a mother knows. You'll see. I can feel that my son has left this turbulent world. I can feel it. But, don't you worry, Margaret. I can't feel that James Bayless left us, too."

Maggie sighed with relief, in spite of herself. "I have brought a nice lunch and some sweet tea for us, and I thought we might work a little cross-stitch to fill our time."

Chapter 8

Ute Village near Tarn City, Colorado

October 31, 1872

The Ute braves had waited in the hills above Harmony, watching Bayless' sorrel with the red silk tied around her saddle horn. They were curious about the old white man with the great beard who had arrived at the edge of town a short time earlier, and now stood holding Bayless' horse. They recognized him as the wagon driver with the gun, when they were burying the runner's friend, but what was he doing with the runner's horse? Just as they were about to climb down the hillside and ask about it, they saw James Bayless running from the town, flat-out toward the old man holding the horse. They watched as the men waved to each other. When Bayless reached his horse, he shook hands with the bearded man. He must have told him glorious news, because the bearded man threw his arms up in the air and danced a jig. He then threw his arms around Bayless and kissed him on both cheeks. The Indians exchanged glances.

Bayless squinted into the hills, searching for the Utes he knew were watching his back. Seeing nothing, he put his hands to either side of his mouth and yelled up to them, "Are my Ute friends there? Can you hear me? Follow me, to Aria and then on to your village. I need to talk with your Chief again."

They watched Bayless mount his horse and wave away to the bearded man. He steered his mount toward Aria and the Indian village near Tarn City, and the natives followed.

Bayless sat atop blankets that covered the floor of the teepee, feeling the best kind of exhaustion; he had spent the late afternoon racing one Indian after another in short dashes. It seemed every brave in the tribe wanted a shot at the fast man, much to their Chief's delight. Most of the Indians ran in moccasins. After many consecutive losses, some of the braves removed their soft leathers and ran barefoot, too. However, it did not seem to alter the outcomes; Bayless won every race.

 He thanked the Ute-Apache Chief Latuka for his hospitality and took another bite of delicious bread. More than a thousand dollars in gold pieces lay on the floor, glinting in all their allure before the fire. Jim pulled a piece of paper from his shirt pocket. "I wrote this down for you, Chief, so's you don't get cheated out of any of your gold. This much gold should feed your people the whole winter and perhaps beyond." He handed the single sheet to the Indian. "Your men said you are learned. But you tell me if there is anything I wrote there that you don't understand."

The chief pointed immediately to a word he did not know. "That's oleo. I didn't know if your women used that to cook with. I can tell you our white women cook with it, probably for every meal. I wrote down how much just one of those coins would buy of each of those dry goods, too, for instance, eight handcarts of grain, ten pounds of sugar, or twenty-five pounds of salt. They're examples that should give you a fair idea of value."

"You are a good white man, Bayless. Not too many white men are good these days. Your first gift of horse-burro fed my village for several days when we were very hungry and poor. Now again, because of you, I can care for my village all through the winter. We will not know hunger again. You are a good friend."

"You are welcomed, Chief Latuka. It was nice knowing somebody was watching my back so I could make my way to the race. I only wish I had somebody like those two braves watching my backside for the way home—I imagine those traveling swindlers are not much happy about my winning a race they thought they had sewn up. I expect they'll try to come for the gold." He took another bite of warm bread. "And by the way, I think you are good Apache. Perhaps I will meet a few more of your people making my way across the Territory."

"I hope not." The chief remarked. "Not too many Apache are good, either." Bayless laughed at that. "No, I speak the truth. You must have an Indian escort. Stay with us tonight and be our guest. In the morning, I will send my two soldiers to follow you and keep other Indians from attacking."

"Can your braves run distance, Chief? Because it may come to that."

"They are my best. They run long; the marathon. They can cross The Territory in eight days, if necessary." Latuka promised.

"I'm obliged, chief. Thank you."

Latuka nodded, pleased for the friendship. "It is easier to hide among the ridges and rocks, but perhaps not in shoeless feet; the rocks can be sharp. Your enemy's horses would not navigate such terrain as well as you. Keep the red silk in view of my soldiers."

Latuka drew in on his pipe and blew large smoke into rings in the air between them. Then he blew smaller rings through the large ones as they faded toward the open smoke flaps at the tip of the teepee. He looked at his guest and smiled. "I learned that from a blue soldier. Also, he taught us how to play the game, *Jucker*. Do you play?"

"Heck yeah. Everyone I know plays that card game." Jim answered.

 "When we see you next, we must play a few hands." The Chief was clearly pleased. He nodded to his squaw and accepted a handful from her. "You should wear these on your journey." He turned back to Bayless, placing a gift on the floor between them. "They are meant for the long run, the marathon. They are not so much for fast running—we now believe barefoot is best for that."

It was a pair of simple, drawstring leather spats, with a pair of moccasins unlike any Jim had seen before. Made from exceptionally soft but durable leather, the soles were double thick and hand-stitched to the vamps. The vamps were much longer than most running shoes or moccasins, with holes for the leather ties punched all the way to the top of the shoes, which cut just below the anklebone. The extra-long laces began all the way down near the base of the toes. Bellows tongues allowed the shoes' width to stretch with the runner's strides, but it was the way in which the straps were tied at the top of the shoe that Bayless found most interesting.

Jim pulled the shoes on eagerly and set about tightening the laces, bottom-to-top—they were a perfect fit.

When he reached the top holes, the chief put out a hand to stop him from poking the laces through. "Wait", he ordered. He nodded at his squaw, who scuttled forward and kneeled before Jim's left shoe. She lifted the inside lace and poked it through the top hole, inside-to-outside, then poked it back through, leaving about a two-inch long loop hanging on the outside of the moccasin, but with a serviceable length of the leather strap left over, on the inside. Silently, she repeated the routine with the outside lace. She then picked up the right-side lace and passed it through the left-side loop; she put the left-side lace through the right-side loop. She pulled on both straps, evenly and in a downward motion, over Jim's feet. The loops and straps tightened homogenously, if not magically, about his feet. Then she tied the straps into snug, standard, shoelace-tied bows. The squaw tied Jim's other foot in the same manner, slowly again, so that Jim could recall the steps later. She smiled up at Jim, handed him the spats and scurried back to her bearskin, behind the chief.

Jim wiggled his toes with satisfaction. He jumped up and down inside the teepee and flexed his feet, causing the squaw to giggle. "They're comfortable; a perfect fit. They're *real* comfortable—and real sturdy, too. They seem to give, and yet my heels don't slide up, down and all around—no blistered feet for me," he beamed. "And I've also got these swell spats to protect my ankles and keep the dirt out of my shoes. I don't know how to properly thank you, Chief Latuka. I've never seen a shoe like them." Jim was truly grateful and hoped he'd adequately told the chief so. "I just might make it back to my woman in one piece after all. I have to admit it; I was thinking my chances were not so good. But with your help, Chief, I'll make it back. I know it."

The Ute soldiers joined in on the laughter that time. "No, your chances were not so good at all," one jabbed good-naturedly.

"I will probably wind up owing you for my life, before this chapter in it is done. How can I possibly thank you?" Jim asked.

The chief laughed so hard he commenced a coughing fit. He spread his arm over the glittering gold pieces at his feet. "As you white men are fond of saying, 'Holy cow', Bayless. Do you think you have not yet thanked us enough?"

Doc Benjamin stood before the hotel's front desk. "What do you mean, 'someone checked him out'? What does that even mean?"

The owner of the establishment did not bother to lift his eyes from the register he was fussing with. "It means he had a friend come pick up his things, settle up and drop off the key to me at the front desk. It means your fast man, James Bayless, has checked out."

"When did he check out? What time was that?" Benjamin wanted to know.

Now the proprietor looked up at the men standing before him. "Do I look like some cowpoke's nanny to you? Only time I would remember what time someone checked out is if they checked out late, which Mr. Bayless did not."

Benjamin's frustration with the hotel owner grew. He thrust his arms across the front desk and collared the bald little man, nearly lifting him off his feet. "For your sake, I hope your memory returns, real quick. Now, thinking about it again, are you certain you don't remember the time?" He released the shorter man with a rough push.

The little man now thought better of standing so close to his desk. He adjusted his mangled collar and smoothed his clothing. "There's no call for the rough treatment, men. As I said, his friend checked him out just before the last race started, so it must have been around noontime. But I don't know why you're all in a twitter over it. It isn't as though the man could catch a train to anywhere today, not at this time of afternoon."

"What do you mean by that?" Donny Benjamin spoke up.

The little man sighed loudly. "It means there is only one train out of Tarn City for points east, and it leaves at ten in the morning. I doubt your friend is suicidal; he ain't gonna ride alone across a Kansas Territory full of savages and not too many white folks to speak of, is he? So, gentlemen my advice is this: if you really need to meet your friend, you should plan to be in Tarn City before that train leaves. You will likely catch him there. Now, if you don't mind." The proprietor went back to working his books.

Benjamin turned to face the others in his group. "If he isn't staying here, and he cannot leave the area before tomorrow morning, where is he planning to lay his head this night? Where in hell did he go?"

Bayless insisted on stopping in Aria before heading for home. He couldn't leave Colorado without saying goodbye to Lem. He stood before his best friend's earthly remains and wondered how other folks said goodbye to the people they loved. It was hard, maybe the hardest thing Bayless had ever done.

"I did it, Lem. I didn't do it the way we planned, you know, digging it out of the ground. But I got the gold, no matter. Do you know how much I wish you were here to share this with me?" Jim looked around the cemetery on the hill, and at the pretty town of

Aria below him. "I thought this was an awful pretty spot. There's lots of nice scenery to look at. I promise I will bring your ma here on the train to see you, Lemmy. Or else I will have you moved to Wheaton—that's where you really ought to be, seein' as how you're a son of Wheaton an' all. Then your ma can visit as much as she wants. I will do that, Lem, first thing. And I want you to know that me and Maggie, when we buy our farm on Shoal Creek, we're going to build a little guest cottage on the property and put your ma there, so we can take proper care of her for you, and so she's never alone." James couldn't help himself blubbering like a baby now. "I'm so sorry, Lem. I'm so sorry you ain't alive anymore and coming with me. I am going to miss you, my brother."

Bayless set his hat on his head and gave a final look around. For the first time in his life, he wished he were not always in such a hurry. But it was just after sunrise, the sun was up, and there was no time to waste. He needed to get on the trail ahead of Doctor Benjamin and his band of crooks. He began picking his way down the hillside.

"I need a ticket for my horse." Bayless said. He was at the Tarn City ticket booth by 8 a.m. that morning.

"Where you heading, fella?" The ticket man asked. "Oh. It's the long, tall cowboy, come back already. Where is your ginger friend?" It was the same clerk who had told Lem and he about the history of Tarn City, more than a week ago.

"Me? I'm not heading anywhere. My horse is homesick. I am sending her on ahead." Bayless answered. "My friend died." He added, more quietly.

"Sorry to hear that, friend. That'll be $2.50."

Bayless paid it, and then sought out the groom for the horse car in order to buy Indy special favors...and a favor for himself, as well.

"I thank you for the personal attention. She means a lot to me. I need her brushed down, fed well and watered before her stop in Macon." Bayless showed the groom a gold coin. "I could use one more little favor, too."

"Sure thing, Mr. Bayless." The groom was eager to earn that coin.

"When you arrive at Macon, I need you to get Indy disembarked, as I will not be traveling via this train, and then I need you to smack her on the hindquarters and tell her, "Indy, go get the mail.""

"Indy, go get the mail." The groom repeated. "Smack her on the hindquarters. You got it, Mr. Bayless. I'll take really good care of her."

Jim handed him the coin. "Like she was your own." Jim pressed. "I will be returning for my friend in the early spring, and there's more gold where that piece came from."

"Yessir, Mr. Bayless. "I give you my word. I will take good care of her."

The ticket man remembered Bayless arriving in Tarn City more than a week ago, and he remembered Bayless visiting the ticket booth a few hours earlier that day. Good grief, the man was tall enough to hunt geese with a garden rake and wore the chiseled face of a Roman soldier. James Bayless was a hard man to forget.

"I tell ya, he did not buy a ticket for the train on this day. He bought one for his horse, though." The man told them.

"What's he going to do, run all the way home? Donny complained.

"That's exactly what he is planning to do. He thinks we will be boarding the train after him." Benjamin answered the rhetoric. "Of course there is always a small chance that Bayless sneaked aboard that train. If I send just one of you on the train, it still leaves three of us to pursue Bayless on foot, into Kansas. He's just one man on foot, while we will have three men on fresh horses. This matter will be ended in no time at all." He told his crew, stuffing down his nagging reservations. Kenneth Benjamin and his crew were not cowboys—they were not even Americans. He had a nasty feeling they had met a genuine one in James Bayless, though, and they were about to learn what he was made of.

Bayless ran at an even, easy pace northeast toward Cheyenne Wells. The silk scarf was tied about his neck and his new long-run moccasins were installed comfortably on his feet. Otherwise, he wore only his skivvies with a buckskin poncho tied about his shoulders—the later only temporary, to disappear the cool chill in the air that suddenly accompanied the November morning sun. He stuck mostly to the low rock formations that jabbed from the small plains, just south and parallel to the railroad tracks. For a few awkward moments Jim was forced to run quite near the tracks when, as luck had it, a train filled with folks chugged passed by him. Jim was close enough to make out the astonished faces of the window-seat passengers; it must have been a sight to see him, a lone cowboy racing across the boundless belly of the Kansas plains, wearing only his skivvies and a blaze of red silk trailing from either side of his neck.

Jim's Ute friends and their ponies were much higher up in the hills, keeping watch. They carried clothing, extra water and antelope jerky for Bayless, plus more of the gruel made from parched corn sweetened with sugar, the nectar of ultra-runners everywhere. This meant Bayless could travel light. Once he was confident he had a minimum three-hour start on the troupe, he called his Ute friends down from the hills by removing the red silk and waving it. The taller one was named Kutillo; the shorter man was named Hugo-mah. They were both about the same age as Jim. Bayless referred to them as Kut and Hug.

"No good to journey across belly." Hug pointed on Jim's map. "Comanche scouts patrol the river (Arkansas) from Dodge City to the Great Bend. Commanches hate everybody. It is no good south, too. Medicine Water says his people will never surrender to living on reservations in Oklahoma territory. He tells his people to not make any peace with the white men."

Kut added, "Medicine Man says the Cheyennes had always been free, and they will continue to live free, or die. Now they are murdering white men and stealing horses."

"Guess that leaves north and then across." Bayless said. He was disappointed for the extra time it would take, but he wanted to heed his brother's words and not be so much in a hurry all of the time.

"Hmmm." Kut, the tall Indian, spoke up. "In the north, Cheyenne and Lakota, and even some of the Ute people, have joined forces to fight the white man into retreat."

"Utes, too? I thought your people were the good Apache." Jim said, surprised.

"Not all of them." Hug reminded Bayless, smiling.

Jim stared at his two native friends. He was suddenly aware he was only nineteen-year-old and alone in the foothills of Colorado, with two Indians and a lot of gold. He had no choice but to trust these two Indians. He did trust them. He knew he needed their help. "Huh. Kut, that limits me to cutting across Kansas...where? Not north, not south, and not across the middle..."

Kut pointed to a wavy line with perpendicular hash marks, the map's legend for the Kansas Pacific Railroad tracks. The rails cut halfway between the north and center parallels of the state, and boasted several forts and military outposts along the route of wide-open Kansas prairie. The trail the men would take out of Colorado stretched toward this area and the Smokey Hill River. And once he reached Kansas, Bayless would aim to keep between the railroad tracks and the river, all the way to Junction City. There, the river doglegged left toward Nebraska. Bayless would turn southeast toward Joplin.

According to Kut, the proposed trail had not seen hostile Indian activity in more than four years.

"That's our trail, then, four hundred miles across Kansas. I have a good lead on those tricksters at the moment, but they'll be riding on mounts so my lead will soon evaporate. The good news is their horses can only get the heel and spur for an hour or two, at best. By comparison, men like us can run for 24 hours, if needed. The tricksters' mounts will cease being an advantage after the first day, I'd bet. With only bunch grass as far as the eye could see, and their horses not really tolerating such vegetation as well as mule or oxen counterparts do, their mounts could soon become a decided disadvantage."

He folded up the map. "I would like to stop before dark. It's getting colder and I think we will need a fire. I am going to try and make it to Sharon Springs, or thereabouts. When I get to a stopping place, I will wave the silk and we'll all look for shelter, okay?" He looked at the Indians with eyebrows raised.

"Okay. What is that?" Hug pointed to Kut's saddle pack and a partly visible silver belt buckle attached to the leather that served as Bayless' belt. It was still looped through the runner's pants.

Bayless told them it was a prize for barrel racing in a recent State Fair. He unbuckled the pack and pulled the belt and buckle free. He could see the Indians were enamored with the silver prize. "Say, Kut, whack me off a length of rope, say better than three feet, will you?"

The tall Ute did as asked and handed it over. Jim wove the rope length through his pants belt loops, stuffed the pants back into the saddle pack and tied it off. He held out the leather belt and silver buckle to his new friends. "Take it, wear it in good health, friends. It honest-to-God don't mean that much to me, not if you want it." He jingled it.

Hug reached out and took it. "Friends." He repeated.

Chapter 9

Colorado, near Kansas Border

November 3, 1872

What the hell did he just run into? Bayless stopped and looked around the little clearing. He figured he was about ten miles west of the Kansas border, north of Boggsville, but still in Colorado's low laying hills. There was no town nearby, nor any sign of civilization. The little clearing had one hastily constructed shack with no door and no floor. Canvases from several tents were stretched over the walls and on the roof, which was topped with pine boughs. There was a rock pit with a campfire. A large boiling pot was bubbling and spitting, its lid clanking loudly against it. The pot sat before a spit. On the spit, a large piece of meat was roasting.

Bayless wondered where the owner of the campsite was, and why men's bloody clothing was spread all about the clearing. Also, what was boiling in that pot, and roasting on that spit?

"Who are you?" an oddly feminine voice asked. An unassuming man of about thirty years, Bayless guessed, came through the pinewoods with an armload of firewood. He dropped the load to draw from his holster, but Jim was sporting a shoulder holster and was able to get the drop on the man much faster.

"Bayless. I'm James Bayless. Drop your widow-maker, mister." He nodded at the small pistol the man never had a chance to draw. He removed the grip with two fingers and tossed it on the dirt at his feet. "Kick it over to me." Jim ordered.

The man gave it a weak kick, frustrating Jim. He walked over and kicked it much further. Then he flipped his gun around and knocked the man on his head, dropping him like a sack of grain.

Jim turned around and stared unsettled at the banging pot lid. He had heard stories from some of the miners while in Harmony and Aria, of desperate men in the higher, snowy regions of Colorado, digging for gold in the harsh of winter and running dry of provisions. Jim had a pretty awful idea what was in the pot and he mostly did not want to investigate the matter. But he had to know if he had just assaulted an innocent, unarmed man or a murderer...and cannibal. Rumors circulated about the Rockies that some had resorted to eating their partners in order to survive.

"Aw, holy hell." Jim groaned. He dropped the lid on the ground and stared at the roiling water and bobbing heart. He looked up at the meat on the spit. It looked like a footless leg—a man's leg. Jim turned and retched.

When the man came to, he found himself tied to a tree. Jim had taken his boots, as well. That way, if he got free, he was not going very far. "What do you want?" The man asked.

"Oh, no. I'll ask the questions. Who are you?"

"Alferd. Alferd Packer. Some call me Alfred, but it's Alferd. You can call me Alfie, if you want. That's what my friends call me."

"You mean its what they *called* you. I don't believe I want to be counted as one of your friends, Alferd."

The man shrugged and put his nose in the air. "Because you think you're better than me?" He smirked at Jim. "You ain't even got boots."

"Because it's pretty clear you eat your companions, you circus freak." Bayless had to swallow some bile. He nodded at Packer's bare feet and told him, "and I have boots, now."

"The men in my party died. I was going starvation's way. They didn't need their bodies no more. You make too much of it, stranger. Death is a part of life, ya know."

Jim shook his head. "Well, it's sure enough about to become a part of yours. I found the remains of your *friends*. Seems they had a little help dying, Alferd. Bullet holes in their heads tell the story. Five men, I counted. You'll swing for it."

To this, Packer shrugged his shoulders and said nothing more.

"So, I am going to leave you here, without your boots. You'll probably get loose of them ropes, but it will take you a spell. I think you'll get snow tonight. Anyway, if you try to run for it, you won't get far. The closest town is Cheyenne Wells, southeast of our location. Due east is Sharon Springs. Head in either direction, knowing those towns will be forewarned of your deeds, Mr. Packer. Or you can hazard a different course altogether, and risk dying of exposure or frostbitten and gangrenous feet." Jim told him. He had wasted almost an hour neutralizing Alferd Packer, searching his camp and finding the grisly contents of his shed.

Jim decided he would send the law for Alferd Packer when he reached the next town. But he had not the time or skill to privately escort a murderer to his justified reckoning. He had made a sign and hung it around Packer's neck. It read, "Free this man at your own peril. He is a murderer and cannibal."

Jim retrieved Packer's pistol and tucked it into his own pocket. He shouldered his light pack and loped off, due east for Sharon Springs.

By the time the traveling troupe had gear and provisions packed on fresh horses for a couple of days ride on the prairie, Bayless had a four hour head start. It was near two o'clock when they were finally exiting the foothills west of Cheyenne Wells and heard a woman's cries for help. Doc Benjamin was not the sort to abandon a damsel in distress, even if his disappointment of a nephew did get surly over the matter.

"It didn't sound far. It came from that direction," Benjamin pointed east and slightly north. "Hello?" He yelled. They moved toward stands of Aspens.

"Help me, please!" Came the immediate and nearby reply.

The men rode into a clearing and had to cover their mouths and noses from the stench. A man was sitting against a tree and he appeared to be secured with a rope. A sign was hanging around the man's neck. The men looked around uneasily. The small camp smelled of carnage and burning flesh. Bloodied garments from several men were strewn about. Something equally noxious was emanating from a sizzling, covered pot on the fire. Burnt meat hung above it; large, shriveled chunks had fallen into the embers below. "Indians?" Benjamin whispered to the man. The bound man shook his head no.

"Where is the woman?" Donny asked.

"What woman?" Packer asked in a high, effeminate voice.

Benjamin dismounted and walked over to the man. He read the sign around his neck with obvious distaste. "Did a tall man tie you up like that?" He asked.

"Bayless," the bound man practically spit the name on the ground. "I told him it was self-defense but he wouldn't listen. Left me for the grey wolves, the rat-bastard."

"Which way did he go?" Benjamin asked the vile man. Packer nodded east.

"Oh, God!" His notorious pigeon-blinder, Reuben cried out. He had kicked the vile pot over to stop the further cooking and hissing of whatever it was inside. The lid rolled off revealing a man's heart; it was seared to the bottom of the pan.

Benjamin stared at the boiled heart and then to the apparent murderer, again. "Bayless," he repeated. He looked over his shoulder at the other two men. "Say what you want about the man, but I have to admit I can't hate him." He stood, turned and remounted his horse. "Reuben, cut the human dung loose." He turned his horse due east to follow Bayless.

"Hey, gentlemen, can't you see I got no boots? Give a feller a ride into town, will ya?"

Reuben approached with a knife and sliced at the man's front-side. The rope fell away. "Nope."

Daylight waned. They rode their horses hard out of the foothills and then to the border. There, they had to get off and walk their mounts or risk losing them. They walked another thirty miles to Sharon Springs. It was dusk when the lights of a boardinghouse and saloon came into view.

"Thank you, Jesus." Reuben groaned. "We know where our quarry is, he does not know we found him, and now we can go enjoy a hot bath, a decent brandy, and a comfortable bed."

"We will overtake him in the morning, get our gold, and head back to Colorado—by train, of course. First class." Benjamin told his men. Let's just find out which room belongs to our friend, and we can take turns watching it."

"I'll take the first watch. I'll need a drink or two downstairs anyway." Donny announced. The others were fine for that. "Reuben, get your bath and take the second watch while you have your brandy. Then I will take the last watch."

The group turned onto the main street, an especially wide thoroughfare that turned out to be the only street in the town. Business was located in the center of the street, and residences were at the street ends. A few additional residences dotted the dusty landscape, but they were not on the organized main thoroughfare, and rather looked as though they were randomly set in place by a tornado. In the center of the Main Street, at its widest point, an enormous Cottonwood stood, its four strong arms reaching high into the air. Wagons and horses gave the big tree berth.

The men's boots trudged loudly against the veranda of the boarding house. A somewhat delicate sign posted on a carved door announced the place was somebody's with a Scandinavian or German name. They hadn't the energy to pick up their feet, and shuffled along. Benjamin opened the front door to a sparsely furnished but clean-looking parlor. A bookish man in his fifties rose from a rocking chair where he had, indeed, been reading a dime store novel.

"Need a room? A couple of rooms?" He asked.

"No bar?" Donny whined.

"Across the street, young man. Don't allow drinking in my home."

How many rooms do you have, Mister?" Donny asked.

"I have three, but one's already taken. One of the other rooms has two beds, though."

"One is already taken, you say?" Donny looked at his uncle. "Who might that be, I wonder? Maybe we don't have to wait for morning. I can settle this whole business right now." He brushed passed the manager and took the stairs two at a time. He listened at a door that was closed and, having apparently heard some interesting movement behind it, kicked the door in. Amid a woman's screams and a man's agitated shouts, Donny ran pell-mell down the stairs, three at a time. Shots flying were flying behind him.

"What the devil?" the manager looked at Benjamin.

"That ain't Bayless, and he's pissed!" Donny yelled at his partners as he ran out the door and across the street.

"Stop shooting! The fella is gone. Don't go peppering my house over somebody had a few too many." He told a grumbling customer who finally returned to his room. "That's why I don't allow drinking in my house." The man told Benjamin.

"Sorry for the trouble, friend. Chalk it up to the indiscretions of youth. Tell me, is there another place in town a person can rent a room? We're looking for a friend." Reuben asked.

"Hmm. A friend, you say. No, we don't have much use for a big hotel in these parts. This here, today, is the most excitement Sharon has seen in months."

"What do you mean by that, old timer?" Reuben asked.

"Well, there was your friend there, with what he just done. And earlier a fella came through telling quite a story; got the whole town riled, I can tell you. He said he left a murdering cannibal across the border, and we'd know him when he walked into our town tonight with no boots for his feet.

"I see you fellas have your boots, and it's a darned good thing for ya, too. If the cannibal does show up here, he will take a wrong turn up the arm of a cottonwood, I can promise you—that one right out there in the middle of the street." The man pointed. "We don't accommodate such doings here."

"Bayless was here." Benjamin told Reuben.

Reuben looked around. "Yeah, but where do you suppose he's gone?"

Benjamin had turned in early, immediately after a bath, a shave and some supper. Even so, the sun came streaming rudely through his window far too early. Benjamin was sore. He would never admit it to his nephew, but his long-distance running days were over. He was over forty and feeling every single year. He pulled his beaten body out of the sagging bed and went to the window. What a sight! Sharon Springs' sons and daughters were ganged about a body swinging from the big cottonwood. They were taking turns whirling it about until the rope twisted into knots, then releasing the body and watching it spin in the other direction. When the body stopped twirling, Benjamin peered closer. It wasn't the cannibal. *They've hung the wrong man!*

The Sharon Springs mix-up had managed to get Benjamin up and moving, and now they were on Bayless' trail, bright and early. The men were told over breakfast how the shoeless cannibal they encountered in the foothills had tottered into Cheyenne Wells the night before, oddly paunchy and pink-cheeked for a man who spent two starving months in the Rockies. Three lawmen were there to greet "Alfie" out of hand, thank the Good Lord for the almighty telegraph, and for James Bayless, who had made a stop in that town as well. Now Alferd Packer was ensconced in a jail cell near the Colorado/Kansas border, awaiting a visiting magistrate to try the man for five counts of murder and cannibalism.

The man swinging from Sharon's cottonwood was a member of the infamous William Coe ring of horse and cattle thieves that operated throughout the Arkansas Valley. William Coe had been caught and hung a year or so earlier, but apparently that did not mean the end of his gang. The hanging man was merely an unsuccessful member of the cattle-thieving gang who did not appreciate that the town of Sharon 'didn't accommodate such doings there'.

Benjamin proposed that if Bayless was running, he would likely choose to follow the river along the flat, seemingly endless plains of dry bunchgrass, so that's the path they would take. The ultra-runner may have had a head start, but two things worked in Benjamin's favor: Bayless didn't know they were following him, and they would be on horses. Fed, watered and rested horses. "Enjoy your breakfasts," he told his partners in crime. "We'll have Bayless and our gold in no time at all."

Reuben looked up from his runny eggs, doubt-ridden. "You said that very thing, yesterday."

It had taken them three hours to get halfway to Gove City, a distance of sixty miles, more or less. They ran the horses for the first twenty miles, but when that failed to catch them up to Bayless, they resolved to walk the horses the rest of the way. They could catch Bayless in Gove City. Besides, they did not want their horses spent again, should they encounter danger out in this rough country.

The November sun was still warm on the plains. If the monotonous, endless prairies of bunchgrass made the riders edgy, the fact the river had veered wide of both the railway and Gove City by twenty miles made them uneasy. They were riding straight through Comanche lands.

"I thought our horses were supposed to catch up to this son-of-a-bitch," Reuben griped.

"These plains narrow substantially after Gove City, leaving little space to run between the water and the rails. We'll catch him then," he said with a confidence he didn't completely embrace.

"So, another day's ride across the scenic state of Kansas?" Reuben asked rhetorically. "Yessir, no time at all."

Benjamin chose to ignore the jab. He squirmed in his saddle. Abruptly, as if thinking about Indians had the power to conjure them up, two warriors in buckskins stood atop rocky bluffs across the river and shook lances at the men. They could just make out the sound of war-whoops. And then,

Bang! Bang! Bang!

Benjamin and Reuben both turned in their saddles to see the smoke exiting Donny's gun.

"What did you do, you foolish, utterly senseless dolt? Do you know you've just killed us?" Reuben screamed at the insolent runner.

"I put a scare in 'em. That is what I did. They'll think twice about harassing us now. You're welcome." He bowed theatrically.

"I didn't see either of them so much as flinch, Donny. But you've managed to put a scare in me. Reuben's right. You have just placed us in grave danger. We could very well become the bloodstains of a forgotten Indian skirmish, somewhere on the great plains of Kansas; the fodder of a dime store novel."

"Well isn't this more fun than shit on a blanket? Many thanks, you execrable little dullard." Reuben drank from his canteen. His mouth had gone dry as sand.

"Say that again, Reuben." Donny aimed his six-shooter at the partner.

"Whoa. Stop it now. Donny, put the damn thing away. Haven't you done enough damage?" To Reuben, Benjamin apologized. "We have been friends for a long while. Yes, I am afraid my nephew's reckless impulse has imperiled us all to savages. I am the one who brought Donny into our group. I apologize for all of it."

The friend could only nod, glowering all the while at Donny.

"Go easy on your water, Reuben. I want some space between the river and those rocks before we refill them again…and we are a ways from any civilization." Benjamin warned.

Chapter 10

Wheaton, Missouri

November 10, 1872

"Do you believe it?" John Bayless asked his father.

"No, and neither should you. Good gravy, an old woman has a bad dream and we should all just accept that it is a prophecy? It's farcical."

John chewed on that with his bacon. "That's true...but then, we are talking about Griselda Hassen, and we are talking about Lem—the same Lem who vandalized the bronze statue in our town square last April Fools Day."

At that, John Sr. raised his eyebrows, wagged his head a bit and shrugged. He did not reply.

"He punched a hole in the top of the General's horse and filled it with buckets of water. Then he drilled a tiny hole in the area of its genitals. The horse peed for a week," John chuckled. An awkward silence passed before Jim's older brother asked his father, "do you think Jim's in trouble?" His unease was nearly a palpable thing.

They spent the night in Gove City, north of the river and the railway, and in the morning, they left for Fort Hays. They rode nearly the whole distance in half a day, placing them close to the fort and within striking distance of Russell, Kansas, but no closer to James Bayless.

"I haven't even seen another animal, let alone Bayless. There's not a buffalo, not an antelope, not a bobcat." Donny complained.

"You should be glad we ain't seen any other animals, since that includes those Indians you likely pissed off more than scared off. They're probably stalking us right now." Reuben bemoaned.

"What are you worried about, baldy? They ain't going to scalp your dome head. Where's the trophy in that?" Donny snapped.

Reuben just gave Benjamin a look that said he was about fed up. "The bluffs are miles back from the water now, and the north bank is just down the other side of this hill. I'm going to go refill my canteen and put some cool water on my bald head." He told his friend.

"We will all go." Benjamin offered.

"That's okay, boss. We are utterly alone out here. Hand me your canteen and I'll fill it for you. You stay with the horses." Reuben dismounted and traded the reins to his friend for a near-empty canteen.

"Donny, get off your duff and help him." Benjamin ordered.

The insolent young man slid off his saddle and handed the reins over, pulling his canteen from the saddle. He trudged silently behind the bookmaker. At the water, Reuben knelt and uncapped the first canteen. He held it under the water until the bubbles ceased and handed it and the lid over to the kid. He dunked the second canteen. Squinting across the way he commented, "sure wish there wasn't such a steep bank on that side of the water, too. I'd feel better knowing nothing—or nobody, was crawling up that bank to get a peek at us." The two men glanced in tandem at the south bank. Then realizing they were spooking themselves, they started laughing, shaking their heads. Reuben traded the second canteen to the kid, who capped it and threw it around his neck with the other. Reuben lowered himself and the last canteen to the water.

Donny looked about for the source of a strange sound. It was a faint, fast twirling sound: *thop-thop-thop-thop-thop.* "Did you hear that, Reuben? Like maybe a large flying bug, or a child's drum toy?" He looked down at his partner. Reuben was frozen in position, kneeling on just his one knee, one hand and a canteen submerged beneath the water...and a tomahawk sticking out of his forehead. *Thop-thop-thop*— the sound approached again. Donny did not wait to see where this one landed. He scrambled up the north bank, screaming, "Indians!" The hatchet buried itself in the bottom of his right boot heel. Donny pulled it free and ran like hell for his horse, the canteens clanging viciously against his chest.

Benjamin was jolted out of a lazy afternoon half-sleep by the screams of his nephew. "Go! Go!" Donny was yelling at him and waving an Indian tomahawk. Then the younger man was on his horse and nearly passing his uncle before Benjamin understood what was happening.

"Where's Reuben?" He yelled at Donny.

His nephew just shook his head no, and screamed, "Ride!"

Down at a lip of the river, Bayless waved his red silk in a wide circle. Soon he had two Indian friends at his side. "How are you fellas doing out here?" He asked. The Ute's shrugged, not sure how to answer. "Stupid question. What I meant was, are you hungry? I brought you some food from the town of Russell. It's a pretty big town. They have a pintsize café that makes these little cakes. I tell you true, fellas, after a few days on dried corn in syrup, I was ready for some real food. I can't stop eating' these things." He opened a kerchief to reveal sweet smelling apple cinnamon muffins. "Thought you might like to try some too."

Kut and Hug reached for the sweet cakes. As soon as they took bites, their eyes went wide in surprise. "Good, isn't it?" He laughed. He handed over the whole kerchief.

As the Indians enjoyed the baked goods, Jim told them. "There's all kinds of commotion over there in Russell, right now. Seems they had themselves an Indian attack out near Fort Hays today. A man was killed and, well, not scalped. I guess the man was bald but sported a fair beard, so they scalped his beard for trophy." The Utes traded amused looks but kept eating.

"Yeah, folks is a little upset over there because they haven't had a problem with the natives in something like four years. The Cheyenne and Lakota are all in Wyoming. The Sioux are in North Dakota and the Comanche are in Oklahoma, they said. But then one of the fellas who was attacked had a tomahawk buried in his boot heel, and you know what the soldiers at the fort said about that?" Hug and Kut shrugged and dug into new muffins. "They said it was a Ute-Apache tomahawk. Imagine that. Because, the Utes are the good Apache." He said satirically.

"Not all of them," Kut smiled, apple cinnamon stuck in his wide grin.

Bayless laughed in spite of himself. "Okay, fellas. I think I am going to try to make Fort Harker by tomorrow night. After Fort Harker, I need to dogleg southeast, away from the river, toward Marion Lake. I cannot imagine those two remaining swindlers are going to continue chasing me after this night. If you men want to head back to Tarn City, Colorado, I wouldn't fault you." He handed them each a gold coin. "For you. Please thank Chief Latuka. I believe I am home-free now, thanks to you."

The Indians looked at each other and handed the gold back. "We will see you safe to Mizery." Kut told him. "Chief says so."

"That's *Miss-soor-ee.*" James corrected.

Kut nodded. "Mizery."

James laughed. "No, it's *Miss*—never mind. You fellas want some more of that? I can get you more." He nodded at the kerchief, empty of all but crumbs.

The Utes declined his offer, but rubbed their bellies in appreciation. James shook the rag and stuffed it in his back pocket. "I guess I will see you on the plains tomorrow then, fellas." He turned to climb the north bank and head back for the town of Russell, a tall beer and a T-bone steak.

"You will not see us. But we will see you." Kut told him. He gave Jim a happy grin.

"Ooooh, I'm sorry, I'm sorry, I'm sorry!" Maggie exclaimed. The buck wriggled in her lap. She had him on his back and was clipping his nails. She had daydreamed—a wonderful daydream about what it would be like to be married to James Bayless and bear his children, but she clipped the nail to short and now it was bleeding and probably hurt a good deal. She kept a little pot of alum nearby, just in case. She rarely had to use it, but for poor Elmo, it would be necessary today. She dipped his paw into the pot and held pressed alum to the injured claw. Elmo ceased his squirming and Maggie continued on with the other paws. She wasn't at it for long before her father ambled down the sloping acreage to her rabbit barn and told her to put the rabbit away.

"But father, I have so many that I still need to—" She noted the look on her father's face. "Yes, sir." She grabbed the bunny by his ears and tucked him against her like she was stealing bread; it kept the rabbit from kicking at her with back claws that could rip skin quite efficiently. She locked the cage and turned to her father.

"What is this about?"

"I don't want you to get upset."

"I won't." She answered decisively.

Her father stared at her for a long time before he continued. "There's been some commotion in town, at the mercantile. The Bayless family is already there. You should go." His face betrayed his fear. He feared his daughter's heart was about to be broken.

"Commotion…?" Maggie repeated. She watched her father for some sign of what was going on. "Daddy, you're scaring me."

Her father breached the distance between them and put his around his little Maggie. He didn't want anything to harm her, or the life she was carrying. He whispered in her ear. "Whatever you find just remember, you are my daughter. You are strong. You can weather it, no matter what. And your daddy will always be here for you." He stroked her hair. For Maggie that only made it worse. Now she was really worried.

"What is it, father? Just tell me." She broke his embrace and searched his face.

He squared his shoulders and took a deep breath. He let it out, slow. "James Bayless' horse arrived at the Mercantile today, ready to fetch the mail."

"That means he's home! Jim is home!" Maggie's heart soared, before she noted the constipated look her father still wore. "But that's not good news because..." She raised her eyebrow.

"Her rider was not with her." Her father said. He could not meet her eyes.

Maggie was motionless, her body freezing her in place. She could not find her voice, either. Silent seconds ticked by at an excruciating rate.

"Maggie?" Her father looked truly worried. "Your color...are you going to faint?"

Movement and voice came crashing back into her. "I'll go to the Mercantile and find out what I can." She kissed her father on the cheek and scurried down the hill to Main Street.

Many people were out for a stroll, it seemed. She saw a wagon pull up in front of the Mercantile, while another was loading up supplies and fixing to leave. A small group of older women— ladies with children grown enough for them to get away to town for a short spell in the afternoons, stood nearby the dry goods store visiting one another. She nodded to a farm couple sitting on the bench outside the shoe repair, but her pace did not slow until she reached the crowd of men milling about a small area in front of the "Merc". They talked in low tones. As the men noticed Maggie, they parted like the Red Sea. She could see the backside of just one man standing between her and a familiar horse. Jim's older brother John was brushing the lathered sorrel out, but turned when the scene grew still. "Maggie...this doesn't mean a thing," he started.

She pushed her way to the horse. When Indy saw Maggie she turned her head and dipped it lower for nuzzles. Maggie's breath got caught in her throat as she dutifully stroked the mare's nose. She turned to John, tears already welling. She whispered, "John, what is going on?"

"This doesn't mean there is a problem with Jim, not necessarily. As I was just telling these fine folks, Indy would have gone straight to our home if she were merely a riderless horse returning on her own. She didn't do that; she came here to get the mail. That would have been an order only Jim knows to give, which obviously means he is alive." John told her.

"Sure, but when did he give her the order? That horse looks like she's been run hard for two days and nights." One of the townsfolk offered.

"Come on now, gentlemen. An Indian pony cannot even run for two days straight. Sure, she's been run hard, but not too hard. Indy here looks to be fine. No need for anyone to say anything to Griselda Hassen."

"Did you check her over? Does she have wounds or is she carrying a note from Jim?" Maggie asked. There was so much naked hope delivered with the question, it made John wince.

"I did search her and all of her packs. They're empty. But you know Jim. The darned fool probably wanted to run home from Colorado."

She leaned into John Bayless and whispered, "Then, where is Lem? Lem doesn't run distance."

John hesitated only a moment, but he did hesitate, Maggie noticed. "Lem is probably on Riff, riding right alongside Jim. I don't believe the two of them would have split up, do you? Now, now, Maggie, please don't cry."

"I'm not." She sniffed. She looked up and saw the smiling face of Silas Biggs. She froze, but only for an instant. Then Maggie gave herself a mental slap across the cheek, calling back her tears and strengthening her resolve. She turned back to Jim's brother. "I know Jim is fine. He would have sent a note with Indy if anything were wrong. I am certain Jim is on his way home." She said a bit louder than needed for the small gathering, and a little more confident than she felt. *Smile on that, you old buzzard*, she said mentally to Silas Biggs and his highly inappropriate joyous expression.

"Good afternoon, Silas." Preacher Morris looked up from his writing. "What can I do you for, neighbor?"

Silas trudged across the hardwood floor of the little church, tracking clods of dirt behind him. "Guess you probably heard about James Bayless' horse returned to Wheaton without him."

Daniel Morris nodded, surprised at how quickly Biggs came calling about the matter—mere hours after Bayless' riderless horse returned to town.

"Well, now I may be jumping the gun here, but December first is this side of the bend—mere days away. Maggie will be showing soon, and I think we both know hope and prayer ain't gonna bring James Bayless back. The man is done—fallen on some random plain, somewhere in the middle of Kansas." Biggs stated flatly.

"I don't know that, in actuality." Morris replied.

"Aw, come on, Preacher. Let's face reality like men. I am not saying we should move the date up. But I am saying we should go ahead and plan the ceremony for the first possible moment—December 1. I think we should have the wedding planned to go off on that day, if Bayless doesn't return."

Morris thought about that. He wanted to believe James Bayless was still alive. Not only for Maggie, but because James was a good-hearted person and the preacher genuinely liked the young man. But he was a young man without prospects. Morris also did not want to believe Bayless was dead, partly because he would feel entirely responsible. But this matter wasn't about him. It was about Maggie. Biggs said he wouldn't take her in the "condition" she was in, after the first of December. That deadline was just three days away. What would become of his daughter if Bayless failed to return and Biggs passed her up, with a pregnancy growing within her?

"Perhaps it would be prudent to have some of the wider details hammered out—."

The screech of the chair against the wood floorboards drowned the preacher out. Biggs cut him off anyway. "Knew you would see things my way on this, Daniel. I've made some notes here," he dug paper from his pocket."

Chapter 11

Near Russell, Kansas

November 28, 1872

The men plotted how to get a jump on Bayless over fried prairie chicken, masher potatoes and cobs of corn. They were seated at an entirely too frilly dinner table in a little town café near Fort Hays. It was the town's only restaurant, and was obviously owned by a woman. Benjamin was a tall man with hands and feet to match. The fragile looking plate and dainty china cup with the tiny finger trap for his grip annoyed him.

"Enjoy that beer, Donny. I'll not be buying any more for you. We must tighten our belts and keep them tight, from here on," Benjamin told his nephew. He mopped up rich gravy with a fresh roll and took another bite.

They knew Bayless was aiming one town further than he estimated his chasers could reach before nightfall, and they knew he started out at daybreak.

"Isn't that special? Crossing the dusty plains and a man cannot even get a beer to drive the sand from his parched throat at the end of the long day." He grumbled.

"Sure you can. And that one's it." Benjamin scowled at Donny. "Now listen up. We can leave for Russell, that's a town about half the distance to Fort Harker, a little before sunrise—not pitch-black, mind you, but before sunrise. Our horses could cover the forty miles in less than ninety minutes if we ride them hard. Then we will find and overtake Bayless on the trail. I figure we'll have him in our grip—."

"Please do not say, 'in no time at all'." Donny sniped.

"We'll have him within a couple of hours, I was going to say."

"And our gold."

"And our gold, of course." Benjamin was growing exasperated with his only brother's only child.

 "And then we can afford more steak and beer." His nephew shoveled potatoes and gravy into his mouth.

Jim got an even earlier start the morning he left Russell. The sky was deeply bruised with a blood red ball of fire rising beneath it. Late fall on the plains was mild, and the ever-blowing wind felt good on Jim's skin. He ran easily up and down gentle hills of waving green and gold tallgrasses. It looked like a divine hand was smoothing a blanket of shimmering velvet. This was Jim's favorite time of the day, the time—and the sights, that most people missed out on. He slaked his thirst when the Smoky Hill River came near and followed the trail again; he guessed he was about 15 miles west of Fort Harker and the nearby town of Ellsworth.

Jim was alone on the plains, as far as he could see. He stripped quickly, rolling his clothing into his knapsack, and waded into the gentle water. He washed hurriedly, then dunked his head under the current and gave his hair a good tousling. Shy a towel of any sort, Jim donned the knapsack and set out at a gentle pace to air dry under a purple morning sky.

"I think I see 'im. He's that way." Donny pointed. They could just make out a man's silhouette on the plain. It had to be Bayless, though he was far south of where Benjamin expected to see him. The runner was just a dot on the distant landscape, but it had to be Bayless. He was obviously making for Marion Lake.

"All is going according to plan." Benjamin shouted to his nephew. And it was…except for the Indians.

Bayless was about twenty miles from Ellsworth, running easy over a wide flat valley that bordered the rolling Flint Hills, when he thought he heard and felt the pounding hooves of his Ute friends. Whoever it was, they were riding hard from some distance behind him. He slowed to turn his head and look. *Nope. Those are definitely not my Ute friends.* Bayless concluded. That meant it was likely the two remaining charlatans who had been dogging him since he left Harmony.

They knew they finally had him, too; Bayless could not outrun horses, not unless the distance was 100 yards and involved a barrel turn. *How ironic. Out on this wide breadth of prairie, I have no place to run*, he thought. He wondered if the men would kill him when they learned he had entrusted his fortune, save a couple of coins for his travel, to the two Ute-Apache who killed their friend. Probably. *Whelp, I've never been a quitter and I'm not about to start. It may be futile to run, but run I will, nonetheless. It's what I do best. And, Hell, those mounts of theirs have to be pretty well spent by now.* Bayless prodded himself to run faster, his wet skin gleaming under an early sunrise. He was keenly aware of his nakedness.

Just about the time Jim's breath grew ragged and his legs began to feel a rubbery quality, his Ute friends cut across his path directly behind him. They reached down from their mounts with torches and lit the prairie on fire. The dryness and abundance of tallgrasses coupled with the prairie winds, crafted a wall ablaze. It effectively separated Bayless like a flaming curtain from the Bunco artists following him.

"Pull up, Donny! Pull up!" Benjamin shouted at his nephew. They had thought they were rid of the Indians. But when they gave chase to Bayless across the prairie, those danged red skinned sons of bitches rode in between them and their quarry and lit the damn native tallgrass on fire in front of them. The Indians had named Kansas for the wind (Kansa), and for good reason. That famous wind blew a wall of fire at Benjamin and his nephew, so fast it nearly barbecued them and their horses. They pulled up short, reversed direction and hightailed it fast as those horses could make it happen. After ten minutes they had outrun the fire for the time being. A short time later, they ran smack into a regiment from nearby Fort Harker, driving a water wagon and another wagon full of shovels and picks. The smoke was also visible at Fort Hays, some seventy miles across the low-rolling prairie—too far to be of any help to the men on the fire line, but close enough to want to keep a careful watch on the wildfire. Another thirty minutes, and the two men could see Fort Harker in the distance. Benjamin's horse was the older of the two and dropped of exhaustion first, his stout heart spent. Shortly after Donny's horse realized his equine friend was gone, he dropped as well. No amount of Donny's yelling and pulling at either horse could get them to budge. The steeds had picked their moment, as was their right.

"You're kicking a dead horse, Donny." Benjamin removed the canteens and packs, placed a bandana around his horse's eyes, sweetly stroked his face, and then fired a bullet into his head.

"He ain't dead, he's just stubborn." Donny kicked at the horse's chest again. The horse blew air out his lips and bleated like a lamb. This only succeeded in riling Donny further. He lined up directly in his horse's eyesight, and without benefit of a blinder, shot his horse dead, too.

"I don't appreciate the unnecessary cruelty, Donny."

"It's a horse." Donny snapped. He picked up half the packs and a canteen and started walking.

His uncle followed suit. "That horse is dead because you rode it to death. It gave you everything it had, and that is how you repay it?"

Donny looked at his uncle with callousness. "It's a horse." He said again.

"Your lack of loyalty worries me, nephew. I wonder what you will do with me when I am no longer of use to you."

"Are you a horse? No, you're not. You've got nothing to worry about. Dang, these packs are heavy. What are we hauling here?" He griped.

"Food, cooking necessaries, medical kit, repair kit. The usual." His uncle answered.

"Sounds like a lot of crap we don't need." His nephew said. "Let's dump some of it. Are you really gonna cook on an open fire?"

"No."

"Good. We don't need a repair kit either." Donny started to slip a pack from his shoulder.

"I meant, no. We are not dumping anything; I only packed the minimum for survival on the plains. We will likely need all of it. You have carried it all of fifty yards. Quit your bellyaching and walk faster. That black smoke is coming this way and I don't want to breathe it."

"Come on, Unc," the lad started. He stopped when he saw the look on his uncle's face.

"You think we have money to continue sleeping and eating in hotels? We don't even have enough left in gold to get us both train tickets back. We were only supposed to be at this for two days. Instead, we have chased Bayless three-fourths of the way across Kansas. And now, I think I know why he has managed to allude us thus far."

"How's that?" Donny asked.

"Those two Utes have been running interference for him." He noted the wide-eyed expression his nephew now sported. "Oh, yes. They're helping him, all right, although I cannot imagine why." Benjamin was certain Bayless not only benefitted from Indians setting the prairie fire, but also had the Indians' help keeping clear of that fire. Benjamin did not realize that Indians had assisted them, too. Osage Indians who were loathe to see their farmland ablaze, waged war with an Ute-Apache they saw setting the prairie afire; it probably saved Doc Benjamin's and

Donny's lives. Kut would certainly have set his sights on them, had he not encountered Osage interference.

"We really don't have any more money for food in town?" Donny worried.

"We can afford to spend the night inside of doors, but only if you don't mind sharing a room. I was not planning on having to buy fresh horses today, so yes, we are going to have to fix our own food from here on out. We will eat our salted beef of buffalo, and we will prepare the rice and beans I purchased for us. We will be lean, but we won't starve."

"That's bullshit. Bayless will sleep with his head on his own pillow. He's probably fixing to eat chicken and dumplings right at this moment, and then he's going to pay for it with *our* earnings."

"He's an ultra-runner, maybe the best I've ever seen. Tonight he may eat a nice supper in town, or he may eat porridge and run all night. I cannot do a thing about it, because I cannot guess what Bayless will do next. He continues to confound and confuse me."

"I don't care much where the man sleeps tonight. Tomorrow, we will leave however dark an hour it has to be to get a jump on Bayless, and we will recoup our money." Donny hiked the pack he was toting higher onto his shoulder and glowered at no one in particular.

Kut, the tall Ute, still had not made it to the agreed upon meeting spot, after Hug raced east and picked up a still-naked James Bayless. The two men rode to the Flint Hills, where Jim threw on long johns and his running shoes. The two men waited until the fire was extinguished and the soldiers had returned to the Fort. Then, in the lengthening afternoon, they went in search of their friend.

The scene was one of beautiful destruction. True, much of the tallgrasses on the southwest side of the prairie were blackened by the fire, but they still waved graceful in the wind. Instead of daylight in familiar blues with streaks of red, the lengthening afternoon sky was intense with enough soot to shroud the air in watercolors of purple, black and silver. Long pale-yellow spears of sun lanced the sky and stabbed at the earth. It was an awful, lovely sight.

Hug nearly tripped over Kut's Indian pony. He was dead with a bullet hole in his neck, and thankfully did not burn alive, but the animal also had an arrow in his withers, the shaft burned. A short distance away, they also found Kut. Their friend had been hit with an arrow, as well. His body was charred. He never had a chance to escape the fire.

Hug inspected the arrowhead he took from his friend's horse. "Osage. See, it is flint, like the hills. Neosho Valley belongs to Osage. For now." He told Bayless.

"Why?" Bayless was surprised. His family tree is said to have Osage bloodlines, and is perhaps where Jim got his height and running legs. "Missourian's consider the Osage nation a peaceful one."

"They maybe angry—if they see that we start their farmland on fire." Hug shrugged.

The Osage had been herded to a Reservation in southeast Kansas, between the Verdigris and Neosho rivers. During the Civil War, Confederate guerillas attacked U.S. soldiers and civilians, alike, repeatedly and throughout the west. In some cases, they enlisted support from Southern sympathizers and rabblerousers, and sometimes from disgruntled Indians. A few years back, Federal authorities, via a Captain in the Union Army, asked the Osages to report any strangers who crossed their lands. The Osages did a bit more than that. Hoping to endear themselves to the White Man's government and perhaps stem the constant shrinking of their reservation and farmlands, they patrolled the area. Whenever they encountered strangers, shots were generally fired, and war dances typically followed. It had been that way since 1864, and because no one thought to tell the Osage people the American Civil War had ended, they patrolled the area still.

There was nothing of their friend Kutillo to recover; his body was already burned, his soul released. Hugo-mah gave his friend a Ute song and dance send-off, and the two men dug a shallow grave. Hug told Jim, "We go find shelter. No campfire tonight." Jim nodded and followed his Indian friend back to their rendezvous.

"A still tongue makes for a wise head, Donny." Benjamin warned his young nephew.

"I'll be as quiet as a shithouse rat," Donny answered back. "But if you're worried, then you take the trail by the river, where every little sound carries for miles, and I will take the canyon past the bluffs. One of us is bound to find him."

"Hopefully before those Ute Indians find us." Benjamin added. "Won't be outrunning any Indian ponies with our fresh horses—my horse's name is Slug, and I don't think that's because he's fast as a jack-rabbit."

"I say we find Bayless; we kill him quiet, collect our gold, turn ourselves around, and ride hard for the nearest town with a train out of here." Donnie griped. His teeth gnashed mostly skin from the wing of a small prairie chicken. The fowl were more precisely known as the brown mottled North American grouse of the western prairies. No matter what name one used to call them, the birds were abundant and they were pretty delicious.

"We don't have to kill the man." Benjamin grimaced. A runner like Bayless came around maybe once in a generation. He had no stomach for murdering that talent from the earth. "We wait until darkness, hold him up like highwaymen and we ride away safe. There's nothing more that needs doing. You need to calm down." Benjamin paused, wincing as he watched his nephew eat. "Oust the bones and damn the skin, open your mouth and cram it in." He remarked of Donny's eating habits.

"I'm hungry. I'm hungry and there are no potatoes, no greens, no rolls...there's just this scrawny chicken. How is a man supposed to even take a shit?" he complained.

"You should be thankful we have the fowl to eat. In fact, the American president, Ulysses Grant, proclaimed today, the 28th of November, as a national day of thanks. He called it 'Proclamation 210'. The American people are calling it, Thanksgiving Day."

"Maybe the Americans have something to be thankful for." Donny griped.

Benjamin walked Slug near the river's edge until the water took a hard left turn toward Salina, and later Abilene. There, he took the trail that veered southeast toward Marion Lake. He wouldn't be outrunning any warriors on 'Old Slug', as his former owner called him, but the animal was gentle, and sure enough quiet. Benjamin was confident he could sneak by any Indians that may be camping nearby. If there was trouble, he was well heeled with a Colt .44 revolver on his hip and a Spencer sawed-off within easy reach, but he would prefer not to fire a shot. He also carried a knife.

Donny rode his new mount through the small canyon, which was not much more than a narrow crack in the hillside where natural springs had eroded the earth. He stayed close to the inside wall where the moonless night was black as pitch. The darkness helped to hide Donny, but it also hid the tracks of unshod hooves and moccasins—the telltale signs of an Osage war party. The young sprinter was wide-awake and weapon-ready, searching the blackness in front of him for signs of the two Utes who kept foiling their seizure of Bayless. Never once did Donny see danger in the pinnacles of the bluffs above him. He trotted carefully through the blackness, lauding himself for managing to outsmart the Utes, when he passed beneath an Osage warrior patrolling the bluffs above him. The night warrior could not shoot arrows or bullets at the intruder, because Donny was too close to the canyon wall. Instead, he loosed a boulder just above where Donny stood, unaware.

The enormous stone made some noise rolling down the steep grade and crashing to the canyon floor just in front of Donny's horse. When the Osage warrior saw his rolling rock had missed its target, he let loose war whoops that could have woke the dead. Donny kicked his horse into a full gallop, and for the next few minutes it rained arrows and bullets on him. An iffy way out occurred to him; he had nothing to lose by it, so Donny jumped off his horse and slapped its rear before pressing himself into a fissure in the canyon wall. Thirty seconds later, the Osage patrol went charging passed him. Just as Donny congratulated himself for getting clear of a whole patrol of Red Skins and certain death, the Osage positioned atop the precipitous bluffs rolled down another big rock. The warrior had seen Donny tuck himself into the tight hollow, so he rolled a boulder down the accommodating indentation; it guided it straight to the target. Because of the thundering hooves of the patrol that just passed within inches of him, the young runner never heard the rolling stone careen down the furrow to land squarely atop his head. It quite effectively put a stop to poor Donny.

Benjamin heard commotion emanating from the canyon and he could hear the sound of approaching hooves from the east. He pulled Slug into a thick stand of cottonwoods, tied his neckerchief over the horse's eyes, and held the reins close. As if the horse knew the dangers, he never stamped or pawed at the ground; he did not snort, or so much as flick his tail to betray Benjamin. Benjamin swore to himself if he survived this night, it would be due in no small part to this quiet horse. He would feed him apples and sugar cubes for the rest of his days, and he would rename him, 'Hush'.

The patrol passed close by, heading for the canyon Donny was supposed to be navigating. He waited half a minute before he dared to look up and, just in time, thought he could make out the dark shapes of two men and a horse moving several hundred yards ahead of him to the south and east. It had to be Bayless and at least one of the Utes. Somehow they had managed to evade the Indian patrol on this moonless night, too. Unfortunately, Benjamin did not possess enough nerve to give chase, what with the hostiles so very near. He could not have shot Bayless anyway without drawing the savages back on him. He simmered in barely contained fury as he realized his nephew was likely dead, he was trapped, and his quarry was scampering easily away.

Chapter 12

Neosho River Valley, Kansas

November 29, 1872

The Neosho River Valley was located in the center of the vast Central Flyway, named such because it was a vital flight path for migratory birds. The Hickory Creek pioneer trail followed the flight path because, in addition to small birds, large flocks of duck, Snow Geese and Blue Geese also moved across the plains, starting with the trail. Often times, this provided much needed meat for wagon trains, miners, railway workers, cowboys and Indians. By late-November, some of the birds had flown south as expected. But, because the November weather of 1872 was so temperate, many large fowl flocks remained and milled about the tallgrass prairie lakes: Marion Lake, Melvert Lake, and Cottonwood Lake, specifically.

Using the cottonwoods for cover, Bayless and Hug made it far down the Hickory Creek trail, past the earth-lodge Indian villages with their sod houses, until they made the head of the Neosho River south of Burlington. Many of the Indians from the villages they skirted were out hunting, so the camps were nearly empty, speeding their progress.

The two men had started out at around four in the morning, in total darkness. Bayless had been quite surprised to see Benjamin in such close proximity to him, at the southern end of Marion Lake. He and Donny must have ridden all night to try and catch him. Come to think of it, Bayless thought to himself, he never saw Donny. He did, however, hear an Indian war whoop. Bayless wondered if that whoop was for poor Donny. But it appeared the Osage warriors effectively missed the head shim-sham man, and Bayless was anxious to put some distance between himself and Benjamin. Once clear of the Osage patrol, they ran for twelve hours, stopping only twice for food or water.

She stood before a full-length mirror and stared at the image in white with tears in her eyes. The church ladies tied her up in back and fussed with her lace veil and bustle train. "Oh, what a beautiful bride you will be," they exclaimed.

Jim still has two days, Maggie whispered to herself. She said a silent prayer—her hundredth that day, she supposed. She did so on the far chance that God gives extra ear to folks who try that hard. She also lit a candle for Jim. Maggie was neither a cup-half-full nor a cup-half-empty sort. Maggie was the very beacon of brightness; she was, a 'who cares? The cup-is-refillable', sort of girl.

"I won't do it. I won't say, "I do". I will not marry that wrinkled old devil. I would kill myself before I let him touch me. I swear I would." She shook her head with determination. She looked down to one of the ladies working her hem. "You know his first wife did just that? She took poison rather than be married to him."

The woman gave Maggie a pitiful, sad smile. Her own father had married off the woman when she was only fourteen years, to a man nearly three times her age. "Trust me, you want him to give you a child as soon as possible, dear. That way, if he is horrible, you can make your life around the child and forget the husband. It is possible to gain a happy life from such beginnings."

Maggie turned her head and eyed the window of the cramped anteroom. *I am small. I could squeeze through that.* She estimated.

Mound City, Kansas

November 30, 1872

Bayless and Hug encountered a tiny stream that the Cherokee named Pumpkin Creek, and the Osage called Little Neosho. Hug had ridden his Indian pony through the cottonwoods and then sent him home, like Bayless had done with his horse, Indy. He hoped if another tribe encountered his pony during the long journey, they would feed and care for him. They had not seen Benjamin. It did not mean they wouldn't, but the man was fairly pinned down by the Osage on patrol in those cottonwoods, and he may have been delayed several hours.

It rained most of the morning. The men followed Pumpkin Creek to a town named Mound. Oddly, the town itself was perfectly flat in three directions, but terrain to the west of town was practically carpeted with low green hills. Bayless and Hug had been able to run between the hills and hide amongst them. The town was not named for those mounds, however. Originally named, 'Sugar Mound', the town was bordered on the east and south sides by a long, curved hill that was swathed in sugar maples.

Jim purchased new moccasins for him and Hug at the general store belonging to, and named for, A. Honrath. He and Hug had been running barefoot whenever the terrain allowed, but had donned moccasins for their run through thick stands of cottonwood, on a moonless night. Those miles had torn up pretty good the leather string used to sew the soles and vamps of the slippers together. He also purchased new, Western clothing for Hug, including a cowboy hat and a ticket for the train that left Kansas City for Tarn. Besides the post office next door to the general store, there was no other commerce in the town.

"Mr. Honrath, I am going to ask an inconvenience of you, but we would sure be grateful if we could rent your bathing tub. We have been splashing through the mud for hours. Makes me wince to think about donning these nice, new clothes I just purchased, after running across a chunk of Kansas that way."

The owner of the mercantile leaned across the counter and quietly asked, "both of you?"

"Yes, both of us—not at the same time, of course." Jim laughed.

Albert Honrath did not laugh. He looked concerned. "But, mister, that there is an Indian."

Hug overheard and chuckled, looking himself over in surprise; he pretended he was just finding out he was, indeed, an Indian.

"Yes, but he is a Ute-Apache. Those are the good Indians, right Hug?" He asked his friend, hoping his answer would be something other than, "not all of them".

"That is true." Hug answered dutifully.

The serious shopkeeper looked the two men over. "I suppose I could fill a bath for you. It will cost you a dollar a piece, and I ain't filling it twice." Honrath told them.

"A poke of dust should cover everything and more...and you will fill the tub twice, and quickly." Jim insisted. He placed the gold dust on the counter.

Honrath stared at the gold dust for a few moments. "All right." He picked up the poke and put it in a pouch on his money belt. "I'll need a few minutes. Wait outside, if you don't mind." The man told them.

The men bathed as fast as Honrath could muster the filling of his tub, two times. They dressed quickly, and purchased a large bag of roasted peanuts in their shells, which they would eat while they ran. Bayless thanked the storeowner for the favor, but before he let go of Honrath's grip, he asked him, "is that poke generous enough to buy your silence, too, Mr. Honrath?"

"What do you mean by that?" Honrath blinked. *Good heavens, have I been consorting with criminals this entire time?*

"Nothing nefarious, I assure you." Jim said, nearly reading the man's mind. "There is another runner who is coming to win us. We don't want him to know which way we are heading or what time we departed."

"Oh," Honrath sighed in relief. "Yes, of course." He answered.

With fresh water and peanuts, the two runners left Mound for the border. They raced through the Mine Creek Battlefield site just five miles to the east. Jim's father once told him it was the largest cavalry battle of the Civil War. The two friends crossed the border below Lamar, Missouri. It was time for Hugo-Mah to return to his tribe. Bayless had tried to convince Hug to leave for Kansas City from Mound, which would have saved the Indian over a hundred miles of running, but Hug would not hear of it. He had marching orders from his chief to escort Jim to the border, and there would be no deviating from those orders. Hugo-Mah handed over the gold he had been carrying for Jim, refusing to take more than a few pieces of silver to buy food on the train. He hugged Jim fiercely, told him he would make a good Ute-Apache, and bounded off north. Jim watched him go, feeling the sad sense of loss for yet another friend.

Bayless reached Carthage, east of the Missouri border, less than 40 miles northwest of Cassville, in Barry County. It took him an entire day of running. He had stayed among the crumbling hills with their mostly-smooth contours, which were typical of that region of the Ozarks, and found a cave where he could spend the night. Bayless had an advantage; he knew this area. While growing up, his father, older brother and he had camped and hiked the area extensively.

The next morning, December 1st, Jim rose early and set out for Neosho, directly north of Cassville and Wheaton. He was confident he had shaken Benjamin off, and decided he was going home to Maggie. If Benjamin was still following, he did not know the area, and he could not guess Jim's direction—unless Honrath gave him up.

The sun was pretty high in the sky before Kenneth Benjamin stumbled into Mound to ask about new moccasins, and about any other ultra-runners that may have passed through. "It would have been a tall man, legs long enough to paint your eaves without any ladders. He would have been traveling with an Indian—a short one. They're a hard pair to miss." He told the shopkeeper.

Albert Honrath was good for his word; he held his tongue. "Don't know much about no cowboy and Indian runnin' across the plains, mister." He unwrapped a pair of moccasins made for men with large feet and pushed them over the counter at Benjamin. The stranger wasn't nearly so amicable as the other two men had been, nor has this new stranger offered him so much as a silver piece to rack his memory.

Benjamin sat in a chair to try on the moccasins. He unwrapped strips of cloth that had tied his running slippers to his feet for the past thirty miles. His toes were bloody and his feet were battered on their soles. The Indian slippers felt soft on the tips of his toes and they protected the sore bottoms of his feet. Benjamin sighed audibly and smiled. When he opened his eyes again, he saw something next to an ornate cash register on the storekeeper's desk that he had not seen before; a poke of gold dust. It was the sort of means that many of the people in Harmony, Colorado had placed their wagers with.

Benjamin looked the storekeeper in the eye. "Bayless was here," he told Honrath.

"I don't know what you mean by that, fella."

"Do me the courtesy of not playing the fool, Mr. Honrath, or playing me for one. James Bayless and his Indian friend were here and they left you that gold dust." He rose and glowered at the storekeeper across his desktop.

"An' I suppose you got some gold dust for me, too, if I tell you which way they went, eh?"

Benjamin shook his head. "No. Sorry. I don't have any gold dust. But I have this," he nodded at the pistol that was suddenly in his grip. "Which way did you say they went?" He demanded.

Honrath pointed the way.

"By the way, I cannot pay for these." He informed Honrath about the moccasins, as he ran out the door.

It had rained most of the morning, and Benjamin easily found the tracks Bayless and the Indian had left in the Mound City mud. He followed their footprints to Carthage. There, the two sets of prints split off in opposite directions. He followed just one man's footprints—the man with the long feet, to some smooth-shaped rock formations in the hills of the Ozarks, but there he lost track of Bayless. Shadows were already growing long. Benjamin could only hope Bayless had stopped for the night instead of pushing through in the dark, because Benjamin's feet were in no shape for another night run. He located a cavity in the rocks deep enough to offer some protection and settled in for the night. In the morning he woke early and pushed south toward the next town, since that was the general direction Bayless had been heading.

Jim had moved from the crumbling hills into mild knolls that were thickly wooded. He looked back over his shoulder often, unsure if

Benjamin was still tracking him, or not. He saw nothing, save the abundant wildlife the area enjoyed, and thought he might be safe to run straight to Cassville and on home to Wheaton. Jim was so homesick his heart nearly ached for the idea. But he would not take the chance of leading Benjamin to his family; first, he would climb a tree and look out behind him. If he failed to see any sign of Benjamin, then he would continue on. He sat on a branch for the better part of fifteen minutes—a long time to cool one's heels, and thought he was in the clear. Fixing to climb down, he scrutinized once more the landscape behind him. He saw movement, and then he caught sight of a dark-haired man picking his way toward the end of the rocky hills. Benjamin was heading straight for him.

Because of the recent rains, Jim knew the ground was soft and had remembered his footprints. If you cannot beat him, you might as well join him, Jim figured. He jumped down and began leaving a well-marked trail for the Bunco artist to follow. He veered toward the easterly side of Cassville, to an area thick with karst, above the Crystal Caverns. There, he would shake the charlatan, once and for all.

He chose the particular route he was on because the weather was till moderate during the day, and that meant the sinkholes above Winoca would be invisible. There would be no telltale steamy tendrils licking from the 55-degree caves below, no melted ice on branches overhead to warn a man where not to step. Bayless knew these caverns and woodlands like the back of his hand. Benjamin, on the other hand, had no idea what he was following Bayless into.

Karst develops when water and soil flows through cracks in sandstone and bedrock. It is responsible for caves, lost streams and sinkholes, and it blanketed Southwestern Missouri. The Osage tribe occupied the caverns for hundreds of years, choosing the gentle woodland camps to live most of the time, with annual hunting trips to the Great Plains. Harsh Missouri winters during the Civil War led Union and Confederate soldiers, Baldnobbers, and Jayhawkers, alike, to the rediscovery and use of the caverns. Sometimes anti-slavery folks would hide freed and escaped slaves inside the caverns for protection.

Many of the caves in Southwestern Missouri were mined for Saltpeter, which was used to make black powder. John Bayless Sr. knew of the caves from his service in the Union Army. After the war, denizens living nearby stored food, mined clay for log cabin chinking, and often recreated inside the cave whenever a cool, refreshing getaway was needed—this was regularly during the hot summer months. John Bayless Sr. would take his young sons on spelunking adventures for bristly cave crayfish, eyeless fish, gemstones, Indian artifacts of the Osage nation, and sometimes gold dust panned from the underground, or "lost", river. The cave the Bayless family liked best was "Winoca," which when translated to English, meant, "spirit". Winoca had several sinkholes to her from the woods above. Most, while still deep, did not go all the way through to black caverns. One of them did; through the earth, seventy-five lethal feet to a boulder strewn floor below. One could only spot the sinkholes if spiraling fog tendrils escaped the temperate caves to colder temperatures above. Barring that, Winoca could be a dark, dangerous place for strangers.

Typically, caves and sinkholes are found in close proximity to each other, and sometimes a sinkhole would lead directly to a cave opening. At Crystal Caverns, both were true. Over two miles of passages had been discovered, leading in each direction from the only known cavern entrance. But then again, the area had never been fully explored.

Bayless created a trail a blind man could find before circling back around, stepping lightly, to lay in wait. He settled behind a thick stand of trees, his red silk scarf in hand.

Chapter 13

Cassville, Missouri

December 1, 1872

Benjamin was running rather gingerly, Jim thought. And the man was tired; his hips sagged low and he ran heel first. The man had passed within fifty yards of him without being the wiser. Jim watched, disappointed, as Benjamin managed to avoid the first sinkhole.

Jim had only left his deliberate footprints for a few shakes. They were going to abruptly end in another two hundred yards. Then Benjamin would know he had been lead into a trap, and he would become more careful of where he stepped. Jim's eyes followed the promoter, impressed in spite of himself at the older, retired runner's grit and endurance. *My God, what lengths some men will go to for gold*, he thought. Suddenly, he heard Benjamin cry out his name.

"Bayless!" he screamed again, and Jim saw that a sinkhole threatened to swallow the man. Benjamin had slid down a bit, but was holding tight to a tree root. Only a few feet of his top half were visible. Jim ran to help. He saw Benjamin had a holstered pistol, but not a free hand to access it. "You lead me into a trap to die, you scoundrel. I had no intention of killing you."

"Catch," Jim said, ignoring his rant. He flicked one end of the red silk at him. As expected, the runner-athlete let go of the root and caught it. "Good man," Jim encouraged. He pulled the man forward until he could climb out of the pit with one hand and his legs. Before Benjamin could let go of the silk, Jim instructed him, "hang on to the scarf, Benjamin, and I will too. When I say, 'draw', I want you to draw your pistol with your other hand. I'll draw my pistol, and we'll finally have at it. We'll settle this like men." Jim said.

Benjamin stared at the end of silk in his palm. "You cannot be serious...with less than three feet between us? Neither of us will miss at this distance, and neither of us will survive a bullet point-blank. You're mad." Benjamin sputtered.

"It's no crazier than leading a common thief home to meet my family. I can assure you, I ain't letting that happen, Mr. Benjamin."

"I can assure you, I am no *common* thief." Benjamin retorted. It rang hollow.

"Mr. Benjamin, you lost. You gambled and you lost. I know you like to think of what you do as entertainment, and that you think folks you entertain should pay a fee, but you would be wrong. Those folks agreed to wager their dollars with you for a fair shot at winning more, not buy tickets to a fraud. There isn't anyone else around to hear this. You know I'm speaking the truth.

"I raced your friend fair-and-square and I beat him. But you couldn't accept that, and now you have lost more than your gold. You've lost your horse, your friend, your family...maybe even a piece of your soul." Jim looked down at the silk tether between them. "Or you could let go of the silk, Mr. Benjamin. Accept a gold piece from me and catch the train for home." Jim did not wait for an answer. He flipped a gold piece in the air.

Doc Benjamin let go the silk and caught the coin. When he looked again, Bayless had a gun leveled at his middle. *Well, that's probably fair*, he thought to himself. "Ours was one of the damnedest fights or footraces that has taken place in modern times," Benjamin told Bayless, seeming to give up. "But I suppose it is over, for me."

"This isn't what you think. Hand over your pistol, Mr. Benjamin."

He handed over the pistol by its grip. "You're going to leave a man to cross the great frontier without a weapon?" He asked, dubious. "You may as well kill me where I stand." He never would have taken Bayless for a double-cross. Jim ignored him and dumped the bullets from Benjamin's pistol into his hand. He tossed them into the woods.

"Do you know you're the runner I have been looking for my entire career, Bayless? You're the natural I have waited for. I could train you to be the greatest Fast Man the world has ever seen—my nephew Donny, God rest him, wouldn't have been fit to carry your running slippers. Isn't there any part of you that wants that?"

"Nope. I just want a good, long life with Maggie, Mr. Benjamin. And to be honest, I'm not looking for it to go by in a hurry. I'm ready to slow down."

"Ah, I do not know who I think I'm kidding; perhaps myself. I have wanted to retire my racing shoes since I hit forty years—and you don't want to know how long ago that was." The older man gave a humble laugh. "I would dearly love just one town to call home. No more acting troupes, snake oil salesmen or magicians and their magnet belts to gallivant around with—I want to be respectable. I want—wanted, to promote bare knuckle boxing matches." He smiled a bit sheepish at Bayless.

"You would have a tough time in that career, I think." Bayless told him honest.

"Thanks for the heads up." Benjamin snipped.

Bayless shrugged. "You don't understand Americans, Doc. Overseas, you call yourself a 'promoter'. Here, you would be called a "sport", because folks who gamble on competitions with you expect a sporting chance. When you took people's money, Mr. Benjamin, you were gambling too. You shouldn't gamble what you cannot afford to lose. And you shouldn't cheat; we call those fellas 'poor sports', or 'spoil sports'. Nobody will gamble with you twice. Trust me, you want to start being a good sport and build a reputation on it. That's the only way you will ever realize your dreams here, in America."

He turned and tossed the man's ammunition-free pistol northwest into the wooded gauntlet Benjamin had just run. "The way out is that way. No sinkholes over there." Bayless said. He turned and ran away, never looking back.

"December first, a charmed day. By the end of the day, everything you can see from my front porch will belong to me." He turned from the open door wearing a grin his son found obscene. Biggs stared at his son, waiting for a reply.

"That's really…good, Pa"

"That's really good, Pa," Biggs mimicked unkindly. "If that's all you got to say, then keep it shut."

"Yessir," Buddy answered, sounding uninterested in the conversation.

An agitated Silas put his palms on the butts of his side-worn pistols and tapped the leather sheaths with his fingertips as he stared at his half-breed son. "You know what, Buddy? You don't have to like it. All you have to do is not screw it up. I will be the richest man in Barry County. I could buy a judgeship for myself, I bet. There's only one thing that can stop this now, and that's the return of Bayless. It ain't likely, 'cause he's probably dead somewhere between here and Colorado, but I ain't leaving nothing to chance.

"I got a couple men posted on the west side, which is the likeliest direction for his return. I want you standing guard at the north end of Cassville, just in case. If you should set eyes on James Bayless before 5 o'clock today, all you got to do is fire this Henry rifle straight up in the air to alert me, you got it?"

"And then what? You gonna do something to Jim?"

"Don't you trouble your pretty head over James Bayless. All I want to hear out of your mouth is, "yes, I got it"."

"Yes, I got it." Buddy answered, bored.

Silas crossed the room in two strides and knocked Buddy off his stool. "What the hell is wrong with you, imbecile?" Without waiting for an answer, Silas growled, "go on, get your butt up to the north end of Cassville and stand guard. What are you waiting for?"

Buddy raised himself and started for the door, ducking in anticipation of another smack. "Take the Henry, imbecile!" Silas yelled at the boy.

Buddy had sat, paced, did stretches, and pretended to site down some ducks to shoot. Boredom eventually got the better of him, though, and finally he lay down in cool grass, his head and shoulders propped by a moss-covered rock. James Bayless found Buddy sound asleep and tapped at his boot with his own foot. Buddy stirred.

"Hey, Buddy. What are you doing sleeping on the side of the road all the way up here?" Bayless asked.

Buddy rubbed his eyes. "Oh. Hey, Jim. You're still alive? Because Indy ran into town all lathered up and rider-less, a couple days ago, so...so most folks think you're dead." Buddy looked over at the rifle lying in the grass at his side. "What time is it?" He asked.

Jim looked up in the sky. "Well past noon, I would say. I'd guess maybe 2 or 3 o'clock."

"My pa is planning to marry your girl at 5 o'clock today. He made a pact with Pastor Morris. Pa really only wants the land. Did you know he's trying to buy up all the farms in town that are behind in taxes? If he marries Maggie, he thinks he gets her pa's land for free, but he said he could also use a good maid and cook. I feel real sorry for Maggie.

"I'm supposed to fire a shot off if I see you before the wedding. It's at Reverend Richardson's little Bible church and her dad is gonna marry 'em." He looked up at an amused Bayless. "It's true. You gotta do somethin' for Maggie. You gotta stop it."

"I can assure you I'm going to do something to stop it. Don't worry it further." He chuckled. "You know, I believe that is the most words I can recall you ever saying, Buddy Biggs. Thank you for the heads-up. You're a good man and a good friend."

The approval from Bayless caused the unfortunate, browbeaten man's heart to soar. "Thanks. Thank you. You are too." He beamed.

"Can I ask you, Buddy…why you ain't tried to get away from your old man?"

Buddy stood and brushed the grass and fleas from his clothing. He looked up at Bayless. "I ain't smart. I can't make my own way," he answered, full of shame.

"You're smart enough, Buddy. You can read, you can count and you can reason. You just got a bad deal for a father." He pressed a few gold pieces into the young man's hand and told him. "Hide that on your person and don't tell anyone what you have. That's enough money to get you a fresh start, Buddy. I wouldn't blame you if you picked up that Henry rifle right now and just kept on walking, until you find a place that feels like home."

"Walk?" Buddy asked, blinking at the glittery gold in his hand.

"I'm going to need your horse, Buddy. Can I buy your horse?" Bayless asked.

Buddy stared at the gold in his hand for a good long while. "That's over $500." Jim told him. "Live frugal, and that could last you two years without working a day."

Buddy shook Jim's hand, smiling. He picked up the Henry and without a word he started walking…north.

Silas Biggs had posted men west of town and north of town. He wasn't expecting Jim to head east of town. So that's just what Jim did. Shoal Creek was east of town, and Bayless had a date with a property deed.

He paid the owner of the farm $5,500 for the property, and another $1,500 for a good deal of starter-stock, in cattle. His last stop before heading to the church was a merchant in town, who was said to trade in diamond rings. It was almost 4 o'clock.

Bayless slipped silently inside the partially opened church doors. He took in the flowers, the few fancy dressed guests, and Maggie in her gown and suddenly felt awkward. He was worn and dirty, and no doubt smelled ripe. He figured Maggie would understand. He waited for that all-important moment when the preacher asks if anyone objects to the marriage. Jim started down the aisle, arm raised. He had been about to holler "I do", but Maggie beat him to it.

Silas started to laugh and Maggie's hand flew to her mouth, her eyes wide. "I didn't mean, 'I do', I meant I object!" She looked to her father, her terror evident on her youthful face.

"I do, too, if that helps matters." A familiar, easy voice came from behind Maggie.

"Jim." Maggie's breath was taken away. *Talk about having a hero breeze in at the last possible moment and save fair maiden!*

"Silas," Bayless acknowledged, taking the three stairs up to the dais. "I am neither dead nor poor," he said to Preacher Morris. He offered the deed to Shoal Creek Farm with Maggie's name on it, to the preacher. "Just one thing. Maggie, how would you feel about me building a little guest house on the property for Lem's mother?"

Maggie's eyes brimmed with happy tears. "James Bayless, I love you!" She exclaimed. Throwing her arms around him.

"Whew! That's what a man wants to hear." He turned to Biggs and dismissed him. "You can go now." Then, withdrawing the ring from his vest pocket, Jim went down on one knee. He opened the box for Maggie to see its contents. "I promise I'll clean up right after, for the honeymoon." Jim told her.

"Preacher Morris, now may I marry your daughter?" He asked. The preacher continued staring incredulously at the deed in his hand.

"Yes! You may." Maggie answered for her father, drawing Jim to his feet. She kissed him. He placed the ring on her finger.

Preacher Morris finally found his voice and whispered, "you're darned tootin' you will marry my daughter, Mr. Bayless, seeing as how you've made her in the family way."

Bayless was genuinely baffled. "But, Maggie and I never…"

Preacher Morris gawked at his daughter. "Then you're not…" He looked a little sad.

"I'm sorry, daddy." Maggie said.

Daniel Morris turned to James Bayless. "Let's get to this, then. So the two of you can get to…that." The preacher blushed in spite of himself. "Dearly Beloved…"

EPILOGUE

James Bayless returned to Wheaton late in the year 1872, after a short spell in Colorado. He devoted his life to Maggie, their children, and to farming and stockraising. He became one of the most-successful and substantial farmers in all of Barry County, and his fine farm on Shoal Creek, just northeast of Wheaton, was the admiration of all. *[James Bayless Obituary, Neosho Times, (Neosho, Missouri) April 23, 1936]*

Griselda Hassen raised chickens on the Shoal Creek Farm, and enjoyed both privacy and companionship. She loved her pretty guest cottage and she often entertained ladies from town with tea and games of Euchre. Jim first needed to relocate her son's remains to his mother's personal garden—until that happened, Zelda could not bring herself to use the tea set or gaming cards her son had left under his bed, meant as her Christmas gift. The notecard from Lem, the one so sweet it quite literally hurt her heart, was kept in a beautifully carved Keepsake Box Maggie had given to her as a gift. She looked at it every day for 12 years, until she re-joined her son.

When James' older brother John returned from college as a man of letters, the Bayless men co-founded the Barry County Bank. They proceeded to loan money to neighbors who were struggling with seed money and arrear in back-taxes. Those properties became imminently more valuable a few years later, when the Bayless boys built the Cassville and Western Railroad to Exeter.

Silas Biggs never realized his dream of becoming the richest man in the County. He never remarried, and he never saw his son again.

Indy continued to fetch the mail for some Wheaton residents another twenty-three years.

The End